THE SEEDS OF TIME

by Shamini Flint

Dear Caitlin.

Save the whales!

Shamini

2011

Book One: The Animal Talkers

Published by Sunbear Publishing Pte Ltd

ISBN No: 978-981-08-0451-0

The Seeds of Time

Cover artwork by Sally Heinrich

Printed in Singapore

Printed on sustainably sourced paper.
Part of the proceeds from the sale of this book will be donated
to the World Wide Fund for Nature.

For all the Animal Talkers

-foreword-

We face enormous difficulties as we work to confront the environmental challenges, from climate change to species loss, facing our planet. There is an urgent need for humankind to respond to the rapid changes that are having a negative impact on our environment and our very future as well as the future of our children and grandchildren.

The Seeds of Time captures the spirit needed by all of us, adults and children alike, to respond across the world collectively. It is a call for global action across all nations, all professions and all ages. We can all be Animal Talkers and change makers! *The Seeds of Time*, delightfully and with a spirit of bold adventure, inspires us to believe that, whether young or old, we can save our beautiful planet Earth.

Dr. Isabelle Louis,
Director, Asia Pacific Region,
World Wide Fund for Nature.

-a note from the author-

Dear Reader,

I have to confess I have taken some geographical liberties with Alaska for the sake of the story.

Also, although scattered thinly across a lot of South East Asia, there are no tigers in Borneo. However, I really, really love tigers and couldn't bear to leave them out of this struggle for survival. I hope you agree that it was worth transplanting a few to Borneo for the sake of the story. Finally, the two-horned rhino of Borneo is on the verge of extinction. There are estimated to be between twenty and fourty left in the wild. In the book, however, there is just one of these great creatures left. Sadly, the threats they and the other animals face are very real indeed.

You might like to know that I am donating part of the proceeds from the sale of this edition of The Seeds of Time to the World Wide Fund for Nature.

I do hope you enjoy The Seeds of Time!

Yours sincerely,
Shamini Flint

-one-

Spencer's tummy hurt and his hands were clammy. It could be the Coke and the air-conditioning, he supposed. But more likely it was because he was heart-thumping, gut-squeezing *terrified*. He stole a glance at Dad. Had he noticed? Spencer was eleven years old and he really hated being afraid.

Dad said, 'It's beautiful out here, eh?'

Was this guy for real?

Spencer peered through the bug splatter on the windscreen of the rented hatchback. He knew they were in Wisconsin. But all he could see were the remnants of every kamikaze bug for the last hundred miles.

Dad saw him squinting, joggled a lever and sprayed the window with water and soap. The bug splatter became bug soup and then the wipers made a bug frame for the windshield.

Spencer caught a glimpse of misty, purple hills, green fields dotted with red-painted farms, snug barns and concrete silos that looked like space rockets. Then a new wave of bugs with a death wish wiped themselves out on the glass.

Dad was really excited. Spencer had never seen him like this. It made him nervous. Dad was usually uptight, worried and complaining about something that had gone wrong at work that wasn't really his fault but he was getting the blame as usual. But now he hummed as he drove and his fingers tried to keep the beat tapping on the steering wheel.

It was only when he looked at his son that his brow got all wrinkly and annoyed.

Dad said, 'Spencer, it's going to be fine, I promise. It will be fun to try something new. Do some father and son stuff.'

Spencer did not reply. He was too surprised to speak. Father and son stuff was soccer in the park and help with homework in the evenings. Dragging your son halfway across the country for something he didn't want to do was just mean.

Dad said again, 'Son?'

Spencer felt tears in his eyes and pretended to stare out the window next to him so Dad wouldn't see. He muttered, 'I just can't do it, Dad.'

'You know why I have to take you. Mr. Valentine said I should bring my son. And he's not a man I want to annoy.'

'Anyway,' he continued, impatience creeping into his voice, 'Most boys your age would kill to have this chance.'

Spencer felt his heart skip a beat. 'You don't understand, Dad. I don't want to *kill* anything.'

-two-

Far away in England, Honesty Smith dumped her school bag at her feet and slumped in front of the television. There was nothing better, she thought, than an after-school dose of what her Dad called the 'idiot box'. It didn't really matter that much to Honesty what she watched. She even liked the adverts – especially the fast food ones where the shiny children with perfect parents chewed on salty French fries.

A man in a too-tight suit and a too-short tie walked over and stood directly in front of her television. Honesty scowled and craned her neck, trying to see past the large belly hanging over his belt. He was joined by a short, plump woman with half a dozen plastic bags and a baby in a pram. They flipped channels and Honesty could hear them discussing plasma screens. Honesty scrunched up her toes in irritation. Her television watching for the day was over. For the thousandth time she wished her parents would just buy a TV. Then she wouldn't have to stop at a shop selling televisions for her daily fix as she walked home from school every day.

3

Honesty set off for home reluctantly. Her route took her down the high street of a small English market town. Further out into the country, the lane narrowed. There was no traffic except for big trucks. Honesty always knew when a truck was coming. She could hear the rumbling and grumbling miles away. She flattened herself against the hedge and felt the truck's hot, angry breath as it hurtled past. The cows, black and white and scattered about the fields, did not raise their heads. No surprise there. Honesty knew better than most how difficult it was to distract cows from their next mouthful of grass.

At a stile, she hopped up the old wooden planks that protruded as footholds, sat astride the top for a moment, dropped her bag over and jumped down after it. It was spring. Small bright butterflies, glistening dragonflies and busy bees flitted and darted amongst the patches of bluebells and clusters of daffodils. But Honesty had her head down as she stomped along the path. She would much rather have been watching television.

Honesty turned a corner and saw her house. The boundaries of the property were fenced with wooden stakes, painted white. She squeezed through a narrow gap. The thatched roof shone in the late afternoon sun, golden windows reflected the light, the stucco walls stood sturdy and upright and a low grey wall encircled the small garden. The soft grass wore a garland of wildflowers. The snowdrops that had covered the ground in early spring like a late snow were gone but dancing yellow primroses (which Mum boiled into cures for Dad's rheumatism) and blood red tulips had taken their place.

Her Mum was waiting for her at the kitchen door, wiping her hands on an apron.

'I have a treat for you, Honey!' she said brightly.

Honesty doubted it. She knew Mum better than that. For eleven long years the 'treats' had turned out to be major disappointments.

'What is it, Mum?'

'I've made you chips with your tea!'

Honesty sat at the wooden kitchen table with a slice of her dinner on a fork. She looked at it long and hard. It was *not* a chip. She was quite sure of that. She'd seen adverts for fast food. The chips that people on TV ate were thin and long, golden brown and crunchy.

Honesty said a little desperately, 'You know, Mum. You can buy frozen chips at the supermarket.'

'Oh no, Honey. I wouldn't do that to you. They're not organic and who knows what they put in them? I sliced organic potatoes from the garden and sautéed them in olive oil.'

Honesty glanced at her mother's beaming face. Mum looked so pleased. It was impossible to say anything to change her mind. It would just upset her. Honesty swallowed a sigh and a piece of chip and almost choked on both.

She smiled and said bravely, 'These taste great, Mum.'

'And they're healthy!' Mum's shiny, dimpled cheeks

were bunched up in delight.

Honesty sometimes could not believe her bad luck. Why did she have to belong to such an unusual family? Not unusual in the sense of being very rich or very famous or only ever wearing purple on Sundays. But unusual in a way that was horribly embarrassing for a skinny eleven year old girl with red hair. She knew her family was not actually unpleasant in any way. They were not criminals or evil geniuses. They had no plans for world domination. They weren't even the sort to adopt pets for Christmas and then drive as far away as possible and drop them by the side of the road when they peed on the carpet.

But they were vegetarian and lived on a small organic farm with an apple orchard, vegetables, strawberries in summer and a herd of dairy cows. They didn't own a television and sent Honesty to school in clothes made of hemp. Hemp! Honesty scratched her wrists. Mum insisted it was her imagination but she was sure that hemp itched.

And they had named her Honesty. What sort of parents would do that to a child? It was cruelty to children. Honesty was amazed she hadn't been taken into care on the grounds of her name alone. She felt she could have lived down some of the weird stuff. If the only odd thing about her was her name, she might have invented a nickname. In fact, her own parents called her Honey – which often made her wonder *why* they had named her Honesty when they did not even use the name themselves.

Or she could have insisted that she was a vegetarian

by choice. Honesty's Mum was certainly good evidence that an organic, vegetarian diet was healthy. Honesty sighed. She wished that she looked more like her mother. Honesty's mother had hair the colour of ripe wheat. Her face was unlined. Her irises were like a tropical sea. She was short, with a full to bursting figure like the paintings by Rubens, a famous Flemish artist. (Honesty had seen his art in books.) And Mum's name was Jane. Not Charity or Hope or Goodwill to Mankind, but Jane. It wasn't fair.

In fact, Honesty thought, if she couldn't look like her beautiful mother, she would much prefer to have one of those ordinary mums with bags under their eyes and a stack of frozen pizza in the freezer.

Honesty took after her Dad. He was a large, shambling man with big hands and feet and knobbly knees and knuckles. He had twinkling, crinkling grey eyes behind round, wire-rimmed glasses and a face creased with laugh lines. What was left of his hair was gathered neatly above his ears and had flecks of red in it. And *his* name was Sam Smith.

Honesty finished the last oily 'chip' on her plate.

Mum said, 'I can make chips for you anytime you like, Honey. You just have to ask!'

'Thanks, Mum,' said Honesty hastily. 'I don't want you to go to too much trouble.'

That was the problem with Mum. If you told her the truth, then she went all quiet and sad but insisted she was just fine. If you pretended to like her treats, you were quite likely to get them again. And Honesty was sure she would not be able to stomach any more chips.

Honesty got to her feet. She knocked her hip on the side of the table as she walked past, staggered forward a few steps, tripped over her own feet and dropped her empty plate. It shattered on the kitchen floor.

'Honey!'

'Sorry, Mum, I'll clear it up.'

'I just wish you'd be a bit more careful.'

'I didn't do it on purpose, Mum!'

Honesty rubbed her hip where she had knocked the table. There'd be a fine bruise there in the morning. She got on her hands and knees and swept the broken pieces into a small dustpan. Why couldn't Mum understand that she was just clumsy?

'You're not clumsy, Honey. Just careless.'

Was Mum reading minds now?

Honesty was thin, strong and wiry. But her feet had some sort of vendetta against each other and would stick out unexpectedly and send the other foot (and Honesty) sprawling. That was hardly her fault, was it? Just that morning at school, Honesty had been made to take part in a sprint at gym class. The teachers (well, most of them) had been willing her to keep going. The kids had put money on how far she would get – twenty yards, fifty yards, a hundred – she had ended in a heap of tangled limbs as usual.

It was only in English class that she did well – the one place where not having a TV was an advantage. Honesty actually read books to keep occupied. Because of all the reading she did, Honesty knew lots of facts for an eleven year old. She could recite the Gettysburg Address (which she did instead of counting to ten when she got angry) and could spell – and knew the meaning of – some very long words like 'odiferous' (smelly) and 'ingratiating' (being nice in a gross way).

Mum groaned. Honesty was daydreaming again. She said, 'I'll finish that, Honey,' and took the broom away from her. 'Why don't you feed the chickens?'

Honesty wandered out the back door. The chickens looked bored. That changed when they heard the door hinges squeak. The whole flock of small browny-red hens hurried over, flapping their wings and stretching their necks in excitement. They knew the sound of the door opening meant dinner. Honesty reached into a jute sack for a handful of sunflower seeds and scattered them on the ground. The hens pounced on the seeds, pecking away with loud, clucky enthusiasm. Honesty sat down on the back step and watched them. She envied the chickens. At least they were enjoying their dinner. It was more than she had done.

The hens finished the seeds and peered around anxiously, trying to spot any they had missed. Honesty was not supposed to overfeed the poultry but she felt a burst of affection for them and scattered another handful.

'You don't know how lucky you are, enjoying your dinner,' she remarked to the hens.

The hens ignored her and pounced on their second helping.

'I had chips – they were awful.'

There was no response.

'I don't know why you keep talking to them. Haven't you learnt yet that there's nothing dumber than poultry?'

Honesty looked around. It was the cat. She scowled. 'At least they're not nasty.'

The cat stalked off, offended and stiff-legged.

Honesty watched him go without regret. That cat had spent the last five years swearing at her and lying to get her into trouble. It was the way he kept himself amused. It was true what he said, though. The chickens were completely, utterly, mind-numbingly boring. They only ever talked about food and the weather.

Honesty pricked up her ears and concentrated. Sure enough, nothing had changed.

'Great seeds!'

'I hope we have seeds tomorrow.'

'I love seeds!'

'Nice weather we're having.'

In between remarks, the hens made meaningless clucking sounds, the human equivalent of 'Oooh!', 'Wow!' and 'Gosh!' So actually listening to a hen sounded more like, 'Gosh! Wow! Great seeds! Wow!'

At first, Honesty assumed that everyone could understand animal language. As a toddler, she had translated what the hens were saying for Mum. Mum had ruffled her hair and exclaimed at what she thought was Honesty's amazing imagination, but she had not believed her for a second.

Honesty soon realised that other people couldn't understand chickens, or any other animals for that matter. And also that it was a bad idea to mention that she could. She remembered the only time she had revealed her talent at school – to a girl whom she thought was her friend. The girl hadn't believed her, of course. It hadn't stopped her telling every single person she knew. The story spread like wildfire. Honesty was called Dr. Doolittle for a month and had to pretend she'd been joking all along. Five years later, there were still a few boys who would cluck or moo when they saw her and demand a translation. No, Honesty had learnt her lesson. She was not going to mention her peculiar skill to anyone – family, friend or foe.

Honesty sighed. Her report cards at the end of each year always accused her of daydreaming and being a loner. Honesty knew it upset her parents. But what choice did she have? Who would play with someone who only wore clothes made from puke-coloured natural fibres, didn't have a television and claimed to be able to talk to chickens?

She listened to the chickens again.

'It might rain.'

'Do you think it might rain?'

'I do!'

'Me too!'

'Great seeds.'

'Oooh, wow, gosh!'

-three-

In a rainforest deep in the heart of Borneo, the orang utans gathered for a meeting. They used their long, powerful fingers and toes to grip the branches – always careful to hold on with at least two of their limbs – as they picked their way through the trees. Big, old orang utans, their faces jowly, wrinkled and knowing, grunted to each other in greeting. Mothers, with their young clinging to their bellies, sat a polite distance away. The babies, two inquisitive round eyes and bright orange fur, peeped out shyly. Males pranced about, sizing each other up.

The gathering was called to order by Orang Tua, an orang utan so old that his fur only remained in patches. Tufts of dark maroon hair stuck up from his scalp. His eyes, sunken in a dark leathery face, glinted with intelligence. He was so heavy he could no longer cross the gaps between trees and had to climb down and then back up to get from tree to tree. His movements were slow and careful (or arthritic, whispered some of the younger orang utans, but never to his face).

Orang Tua let out a series of gravelly, burbling grunts that built up to a roaring crescendo. He shook the branches around him violently. It was the orang utan way to call a meeting to order.

When he had their attention, he announced, 'The time has come for action.'

A ripple of fear and excitement ran through the crowd. Mothers hugged their babies closer and male orang utans bared their teeth and screeched.

Orang Tua scratched a patch of fur on his chest and looked around at his audience.

'Our survival depends on it,' he continued. 'We have run away. We have moved deeper into the jungle seeking new homes. We have gone hungry. We have seen our young trapped in trees as flames licked the branches. We have drowned in the rivers trying to escape. We have watched the many-toothed machines cut through the trunks of the oldest trees. And we have done nothing. But now, I believe, the time has come for action.'

'But why now, Orang Tua?' asked a young mother timidly.

Orang Tua settled himself more comfortably on a broad branch, his pot belly resting on his thighs. He exhaled gustily. He had made decisions that would affect them all. The weight of responsibility was heavy on his shoulders.

He said slowly, 'We, the orang utans, are on the brink of extinction. But this is not a reason to fight.'

There was an exclamation, quickly smothered by one of

the more aggressive males, Geram.

Orang Tua responded, 'That causes you surprise? I understand that. But I am the keeper of the Collective Memory of the orang utans. So I know that what may seem important to us now may not be so.'

The faces turned towards him showed doubt.

'You do not believe me? I will tell you a story,' the old ape said.

'There was a time when giant lizards roamed the earth. Their necks were so long that they could nibble the leaves at the top of the canopy. The meat-eaters were as big as three full-grown mango trees. Some had spikes on their backs or faces. Others wore leathery body armour. They had horns like a giant rhino and teeth like a giant crocodile. There was nothing that could challenge their domination. The earliest apes hid from them and feared them. But we are here and they are gone. And who is to say that is not fitting?

No, our extinction, if that is what Nature demands, is not a cause for complaint. Sadness, yes ...'

He paused for a moment and they all sensed the great emptiness of the rainforests if the orang utans were no more.

A mother whimpered and squeezed her child tight. The baby orang utan squealed and struggled to get free, falling from her grasp and catching himself with thin, looping fingers around a handy branch. The clan laughed and even Orang Tua smiled.

'But if that is how you feel, why do you say we must fight?' asked Geram.

Orang Tua stood up on his short, bowed legs. He held on to a branch with his long arms. His skin sagged and his fur was ragged but the wisdom etched in his face was compelling.

'I do not believe our time has come. I do not believe that the end of our kind is written in the stars. What happens to us now is written only in the book of Man. It is not the will of Nature. It is the will of Man who sets himself above Nature. He is not content to be the dominant species within Nature as the dinosaurs once were. Man is determined to destroy Nature.'

'But how are we going to stop them?' interrupted Geram. 'We can attack the logging camps. But we will be slaughtered by their firesticks. We will just hasten our end!'

'He is right, Orang Tua. We have no chance against the people. They are more aggressive than army ants and more numerous than cockroaches.' It was Chantek, piping up with her contribution.

Orang Tua said, 'You are right. We cannot fight them and win. But there is a different way – a way that could restore our beloved rainforests in the blink of an eye.'

He had their attention. 'A long time ago, forests grew quickly. Seeds were fresh and full of energy. Jungles sprouted in weeks. Continents turned green in months. Trees grew from shore to shore, across the whole land, in less time than it takes for an orang utan to grow to adulthood.'

'But it is not like that now. A rainforest tree takes a hundred years to grow to full height,' pointed out Miskin.

'And is cut down in a day,' muttered Geram.

Orang Tua ignored them. He said, 'Our ancestors had great foresight. They knew that, after many generations, the seeds of the forests would not be so powerful, that new trees might be slow to grow. But they also worried that far in the future there might be a need for urgent re-growth.'

He paused for a moment. 'I do not think they anticipated the greed of Mankind. Men were just apes in those days! But they did fear a fire shower like the one that killed the giant lizards. Some dinosaurs died when the sky rained fire. But most died because the plants were destroyed and there was no food.'

'So what did they do?' asked Cepat, anxious to get to the point.

'They hid Seeds from the first days – for emergencies. If we had those, we could re-forest our land in weeks and undo Man's destruction.'

'But that's wonderful!' exclaimed Bagus. 'What are we waiting for? Let's get the Seeds.'

Orang Tua had not finished. 'Generations have passed. Our ancestors' bones have turned to dust. Continents have moved with a grinding and gripping so profound that even the gods heard them. Oceans have dried up and new ones have flooded the plains. We ourselves are on an island where once we were part of the whole.'

'What are you getting at, Orang Tua?' asked Geram impatiently.

'To put it in a nutshell, our forefathers hid the Seeds where they thought they would be safe, not just for days or months, but for eons.'

'And where is that?'

'I don't know,' said Orang Tua.

The others looked at him in silence.

Orang Tua continued, 'I have a picture in my mind. Everything is covered in white – the hills, the mountains and the ground. There are no trees – not a *single* one. The land is cruel and barren. More of the white stuff falls from the skies. Not in sheets, like rain, but in flurries – bigger than raindrops, but light … and cold, cold, cold. Worse than being caught in the rain during the monsoon and having damp fur for a week.' The old ape was describing the Collective Memory he held for the orang utans.

'But, Orang Tua, there is no such place! Your Collective Memory plays you false. We will never find the Seeds. You have let down the tribe.' Geram's disappointment was so acute that he had forgotten to show respect to Orang Tua.

There was an angry murmur from the group. An old female knuckled her way to Geram and raked him across the face with her nails. 'You will show Orang Tua courtesy. I am ashamed that you are my son.'

The young orang utan stood his ground for a moment. Little droplets of blood matted the fine fur on his cheek. Then he skulked down to show obeisance. 'I am sorry,

Orang Tua. My words were hasty.'

Orang Tua said wearily, 'I understand your worry, Geram. But the Collective Memory cannot lie. This is the vision I have and it is true and right. We just do not have the wit to understand it. Our forefathers would be disappointed in us.'

'So what can we do?' asked Geram's mother quickly, nervous that her son would speak out of turn again and be banished from the group.

'We must call a Council of Beasts. Other species might have a better understanding than us.'

'But, Orang Tua … there has not been a Council of Beasts in … in … ,'

'In living memory and well before that,' Orang Tua finished her sentence for Malu.

'Will they honour the old ways?' asked Miskin.

'It is hard to say. We have grown so competitive for every morsel that our dwindling forests give us. It is possible that the understanding between species has broken down.'

'But we have no choice?' asked Geram, quietly for once, his natural aggression subdued by the enormity of what they had to do.

'We have no choice.'

-four-

Talking to the chickens had awakened Honesty's curiosity again. She had no human friends. Perhaps she should try the animals once more. It would be so great to have someone, anyone – even a farm animal, to talk to once in a while.

She followed the cat around trying to chat to him. Honesty knew that cats were cold, stand-offish creatures but she had not realised quite how unpleasant they could be if one forced one's company on them. And the language! Honesty's cheeks had grown so hot that Mum, noticing how flushed she was, asked her if she was feeling quite well.

Next, she tried the birds in the garden. But they never sat still long enough for her to pick up their speech. What little she could make out was very flighty. A robin sang about the brightness of his red breast. A thrush recited an ode to blackberries. Most of the time, they just hummed and whistled – without words. No, the birds were not much use as conversationalists.

'What are you doing out there?' called Mum, spotting Honesty standing under the oak tree at the bottom of the garden and staring up intently. 'Are you sure you're feeling alright?'

Honesty nodded guiltily. She could hardly explain that she was standing there, head cocked, trying to understand what the birds were saying. Mum would think she'd lost it completely.

She said instead, 'The birds sound so cheerful this time of year. I was just listening to them singing.'

Mum was always pleased when Honesty showed an interest in nature.

She said, 'It's spring, all the creatures of the air love this time.'

'How do you know that, Mum?' asked Honesty, wondering if, after all, Mum shared her amazing, but so far useless, talent.

'What do you mean, how do I know?'

'How do you know the birds love this time?'

'You can hear it in their voices as they sing their little hearts out!'

'Can you understand them?'

'I beg your pardon?'

'Can you understand them … I mean, the birds?'

'Honesty, are you sure you're feeling alright? Let me tuck you into bed and give you some of my elderflower cordial.'

Honesty grimaced as she was fed a spoonful of one

of Mum's homemade medicines. Jane had one for every ailment and was never happier than when she could test a remedy on her family. They always produced startling results because they tasted so disgusting that everyone at least pretended to be better immediately. Unfortunately, the side effect of these remarkable recoveries was that Jane kept inventing new cures. Honesty knew it had been a mistake to ask Mum whether she understood the birds. Positively bird-witted, in fact.

She sighed. She had worked so hard to try and communicate with the animals. But it had not been a success. Listening to the birds had got her a dose of elderflower cordial. She had been ignored by a stray dog, sworn at by the cat and been bored by the chickens. The sheep found her accent amusing.

Her biggest success was with the horses. She found that she could steer them by words alone. Still, she felt pretty silly telling her horse to 'turn left at the birch tree' or 'go straight until the fork in the path'. She was overheard by a fruit picker telling the horse to 'mind the puddle' and received a very strange look. On the whole, she thought, it was more practical to use the reins to guide the horse like everyone else. Besides, the creature never had an opinion on anything. Honesty had tested the horse by picking the most foolish route she could think of from the house to the apple orchard and the horse had not said 'nay' or 'neigh'. He just plodded on placidly.

Honesty realised sadly that she was not going to

find a friend amongst the farm animals. Once again, she wondered if she was the only person in the whole world with this unexpected and apparently useless skill. It seemed unlikely. Why her?

-five-

Elliot Valentine was important. You could see that by the way people behaved around him. They spoke in hushed tones. Some giggled nervously. If someone made a joke, the braver ones chuckled, but apologetically. Unless it was Valentine being funny, in which case they laughed so hard they had to be scraped off the carpet.

The man himself was immense in size. He had been strong but now muscles were replaced with fat. Valentine was so plump that when he walked, he seemed to shimmer and tremble. It was a very odd effect – like the ripples of water on a lake when a gentle wind is blowing.

Valentine was huge but his feet and hands were tiny. He wore crocodile skin Italian shoes that were scaly and very long and pointy at the front. He had nine short, stubby sausages for fingers. He was missing the baby finger on his left hand and there were many tales whispered (nobody dared ask him) of how this had happened. Some said that he belonged to a secret criminal organisation and the price of entry was a finger.

Others whispered that his shoes were made from the same croc that had chewed off the finger. The fat man never explained.

Valentine had a pet wolf. If he was asked, he said it was a dog. But it was a wolf. A pale-eyed, grey-muzzled beast with a thick, rough, flecked coat and a bushy, coarse tail. Valentine called the wolf Tarzan and the wolf would sit on his haunches with his tongue hanging out, looking as if he thought this was a good joke.

Valentine asked, 'Is the car ready?'

His chauffeur nodded, 'Yes sir.'

Valentine scratched his wolf behind the ears and chuckled, 'Good! Let's go and meet this scientist guy and his son, Spencer. I think they're going to be very useful to me indeed.'

Elliot Valentine was soon on his way to the country.

He looked forward to bagging himself a few white-tailed deer. He had a vast ranch that bordered a national park in Wisconsin. The animals were too dumb to read maps and so they often strayed onto his land and into his dinner. The man giggled. Animals too dumb to read maps! That was a good one. He repeated the thought out loud and his chauffeur almost ran off the road, he was laughing so hard.

The fat man sometimes sent his employees out into the park to chase a few deer over the boundary to his land. He did important business on these hunting expeditions. He could not have his carefully chosen guest list disappointed because they had not been able to pot a deer.

The luxury Humvee gobbled up the miles quickly. The fat man stretched. He was large but so was the vehicle so there was space for stretching. The car only did twelve miles to the gallon but Elliot Valentine, the single largest shareholder of the second largest oil company in the world, did not care about that. In fact, he loved the idea that his big, black, powerful machine was tossing back gallons of petrol the way he did fine brandy. Great people and great machines both needed exactly the right sustenance to maintain top performance. Valentine liked the sound of that thought. It was very profound. He repeated it out loud. His driver knew better but the new aide was inexperienced and started to laugh.

Even before he was told, the driver pulled over to the side of the road. A door opened and the aide was bundled out hastily. The driver jumped out, retrieved a suitcase from the boot and tossed it at the man.

'I don't understand?' whimpered the aide.

'It wasn't a joke.'

• • •

It was market day and Honesty was helping her Mum at their stall. People came from far away, even from the big cities, to buy their organic fruit and vegetables. It helped that Mum had glowing skin and shampoo-advert hair.

Many customers saw her and hoped that organic food was the secret recipe for good health and good looks.

Neighbouring farmers were always keen to buy the Smith farm. But Honesty's parents refused every offer to buy their property. Once, Honesty had asked her Mum why she would not consider selling. She could always set up another farm with the money and have a tidy sum in the bank too.

Jane's response was typical. 'The land trusts me to treat it well and, what's more, I don't trust these big farmers with their chemicals and their accountants.'

Honesty could barely keep from rolling her eyes. Just for once it would be nice to get a sensible answer instead of a line from the Zen Book for Hippies or wherever Mum got these one-liners. After all, business was business. And Honesty knew the farm was doing really well. Everybody wanted organic food these days. They were so worried about pesticides and stuff.

A family stopped at the stall. This was the perfect city family on a mission to outdo their neighbours (who bought their organic produce at the supermarket). This lot had made the trip to a real life farmers' market in their four-wheel drive gas guzzler. They were dressed in immaculate chinos and polo t-shirts. Honesty crossed her arms to hide her hemp t-shirt.

'But these apples are all manky, Dad,' whined the son of the family.

Honesty's Mum went into full organic mode.

'We don't select our apples for shape and wax them for shine, young man!'

'Err ... of course,' said the father, forgetting to take off his sunglasses and looking like a secret service agent.

'She doesn't look like it's done her much good,' muttered the boy, glowering at Honesty. She glared back.

'Honesty has barely been ill a day in her life,' said Mum proudly, putting an arm around her skinny shoulders.

'Honesty? What kind of name is that?' asked the boy in amazement, bursting into a loud, braying laugh.

The family moved on. Even the parents were sniggering. Honesty's lips thinned in annoyance. It was a bit much being laughed at by a bunch of city slickers gingerly picking their way through mud in their designer shoes.

Honesty and her mother carried the leftover fruit and vegetables to their car. It took them just a few minutes to stow the remnants in the boot – they had been doing it for so many years. They squeezed themselves in the front and Mum switched on the car (the car had a switch, not a key). There was a loud bang and they were enveloped in a stinking cloud of smoke.

A few farmers turned to stare and one held his nose. Honesty dived down and pretended to tie her shoelace. She *so* did not want to be seen in the turd mobile. This, as far as she was concerned, was the most embarrassing part of market day. Their vehicle was a feat of engineering by

Honesty's Dad. He had bought a very, very old, rusty Beetle that he found on a scrap heap. He bolted sheets of plywood over the rusty gaps. He stripped out the engine and replaced it with a motor he invented that ran entirely on cowpats. It was environmentally friendly but stank when the car was on the move and sometimes even when it was standing still. The new engine was not very powerful so Dad had sliced off the roof with a chainsaw and replaced it with an old canvas tent.

The car didn't go very fast – when anyone in the family was in a hurry they took the horse.

As they set off, Honesty's Mum asked, 'Is your name embarrassing for you?'

Honesty nodded briefly.

'I'm sorry, Honey. At the time, when you were born, it seemed like such a good idea.'

Honesty didn't say anything. It was a bit too late for regret.

'And the clothes?' Mum asked quietly.

Honesty debated honesty. And then thought better of it. She could see that Mum's eyes were bright with tears. She said, 'Hemp clothes are great, Mum, a fashion statement at school. They'll all want some soon!'

Jane brightened up immediately. 'That's what I hoped would happen, Honey. It's a wonderful thing to set the right example to all your friends.'

Honesty suppressed a groan. 'What friends?' she could have asked, but didn't. Sometimes she felt like the oldest member of the family.

Mum said, 'I know! As a treat to cheer ourselves up, we'll have chips with our tea.'

-six-

Spencer knew that things didn't always work out the way his Dad planned.

He remembered, once, watching Dad as he came home from his job as some sort of poorly paid government research scientist. Dad had shuffled in with his narrow shoulders bowed. Spencer guessed he'd been passed over for the promotion he was due – again. Dad had put his briefcase neatly behind the door. He'd taken off his great coat and his scarf and hung them on a hook on the wall. The tip of his long nose was red from the cold. His eyes were watery. Spencer hoped it was from the bitter New York winter. He didn't want to think that Dad might be upset enough to cry.

Mum had watched Dad walk in too. She was a New Yorker through and through – tiny and feisty with sparkling black eyes and jet black hair that was always pulled back in a neat bun. She worked as a waitress in a deli around the corner and always got good tips. Spencer looked almost exactly like her except for the wide mouth that he got from Dad.

The day that Dad came in looking so down, Spencer had felt his Mum stiffen with disappointment. Spencer had willed her not to notice the teary eyes. How awful would it be for a grown up to be caught crying? Poor Dad might never live it down.

Mum said, 'Don't worry, honey. These things happen.'

'They gave it to George.'

'Well, it shows that they're fools. You're much better than him.' She hugged him tightly, 'And much more handsome too!'

Dad laughed but in that nasty fake way that made Spencer's heart ache with sympathy. He said, 'I just don't understand why I get passed over every time. George Ransom spends most of the day nipping out for cigarette breaks!'

'Well, you know how it is, honey. This is New York City. Nice guys finish last.'

Nice guys finish last. Spencer could remember her saying the words so clearly. Now his Dad was going on a hunting trip to prove that he wasn't just a nice guy – he could be a winner too. And for some reason, he, Spencer, had to go along for the ride.

• • •

Honesty looked around at her bored classmates. She'd worked very hard on her piece but really hated having to get up and speak in front of the class. A boy in the front row quacked at her under his breath. Honesty glared at him. She'd better get on with it before the room turned into a farmyard.

She said, 'A rainforest is a truly amazing place. The immensely tall dipterocarp trees form a roof of leaves over the whole area. Their unusual winged seeds spiral down to the ground to begin their own fight for survival. Vast, sluggish rivers wind their way through mangrove swamps to the sea. Iridescent butterflies flit about. Short-winged birds flutter above the canopy. Dangerous predators lurk in the low branches and lie in wait in the muddy rivers.'

Honesty paused and looked around.

'Insects hum and buzz and chirrup so loudly they sound like heavy machinery. Rodents scurry about earnestly looking for seeds and nuts to nibble on. They keep a nervous eye out for the sudden swoop of a bird of prey.'

Honesty's hand swept through the air suddenly to demonstrate the attacking bird and the class jumped.

'Army ants march through the undergrowth consuming everything in their path. Pitcher plants devour the unwary creatures that rest on their lips and slide into their depths. Long-armed monkeys swing recklessly through the trees, hollering to each other about fruit-laden trees. The shadow of a clouded leopard silences their enthusiasm.

A massive flower, five feet in diameter, stinks like a week-old corpse. *But* there is no such thing as a week-old corpse in the rainforest. Everything that lives in the rainforest is part of the food chain. The carcass of an animal is stripped to the bone in days by creatures that feed on the dead, by maggots that love the putrid, rotting flesh and by insects of every kind, slurping up the juices through their straw-like appendages. This is the delicate balance of life in a rainforest – a system so intricate and interdependent that the removal of just one creature unravels the whole tapestry of life.'

Honesty stopped at the end of her piece on rainforests and looked around enquiringly.

The science teacher, Mrs. Adams, a stout woman on a perpetual diet that affected her mood but never her weight, looked green. She said, 'That was very good, Honesty. I don't feel like lunch anymore either, so that's good too.'

'It may not sound very nice, Mrs. Adams, but it's quite natural,' said Honesty earnestly.

'Yes, of course, Honesty,' said Mrs. Adams hastily. 'It was just the bit about the maggots which put me off my food!'

That evening as she walked home, Honesty did not see the crocuses swaying in the breeze nor the ripening berries on the hedges. She was lost in a world where orang utans gossiped with each other and reticulated pythons, thirty feet long, lay in wait for unsuspecting prey. She had read that a snake did not have to eat for ages after a full-sized meal of deer. Honesty, feeling peckish just a few hours after lunch, found this very hard to imagine.

-seven-

Most of the Higher Beasts of Borneo agreed to take part in the Council of Beasts. A few refused. The proboscis monkeys turned up their bulbous noses at the thought of fraternising with other species. The leader of the sun bears (sun bears are notoriously short-tempered beasts) threw a honeycomb (with angry bees in it) at the orang utan who delivered the invitation.

Orang Tua had planned to go to the meeting alone but at the last minute he changed his mind and told Geram to come along. The ape was hasty and too eager for a fight but he had curiosity, intelligence and youth on his side. Orang Tua was feeling his years.

They made their way towards a clearing deep in the heart of the jungle. Geram looked around in dread. The canopy overhead was so thick that the place was in perpetual semi-darkness and nothing grew underneath except luminescent moss and lichen. The ground was damp and the mud fetid and stagnant. The air hummed with mosquitoes. Toadstools protruded from the fallen trunks of trees. There was the powerful stench in the air of a rotting carcass and Geram shuddered. Then he saw that it was not a dead animal but the biggest flower in Borneo, the Rafflesia, which exuded the stench of the dead to attract flies to pollinate it.

Orang Tua too had seen the enormous flower with its five mottled petals. He shook his head.

'What's the matter?' asked Geram nervously.

'That flower. It's a bad omen. We will have our meeting with the stink of death in our nostrils.'

The Higher Beasts arrived one by one.

A vast reticulated python, which must have been at least twenty-five feet long with intricate geometric markings along its body, slithered into the clearing. Geram watched it fearfully, fighting the urge to flee. The snake twisted its mottled body into a loose coil and settled down to watch the others arrive. Geram noticed with relief that the snake had a massive bulge halfway down its length. It had recently fed. Geram did not know which poor creature had just had the life squeezed out of him and been swallowed whole. But he knew the python would not be looking for another meal, at least not for a while.

A fully-grown tiger padded into the clearing on his great paws. His glossy orange and black stripes blazed in the half-light. Orang Tua was confident that the big cats would cooperate in the quest. The tigers were in even worse shape than the orang utans. Like the orang utans, their habitat was virtually destroyed. But they had also been hunted to the brink of extinction by poachers. Their skins were prized as rugs and various tiger body parts were used in medicines. The tiger, however, was putting on a show of indifference. He sat up like a gigantic household cat and washed his face with his paws, vicious claws neatly retracted.

Next to arrive was the pygmy elephant. He marched in and trumpeted loudly. He was the first creature to acknowledge that he shared the space with his natural enemies. Orang Tua and Gajah, the elephant herd leader, were old acquaintances and the elephant moved over to stand by the grizzled orang utan.

'Has it come to this, then?' asked Gajah quietly.

Orang Tua ran his fingers through the remaining clumps of hair on his head, 'I don't think we have much choice *or* much time.'

Gajah swung his trunk from side to side. It was a nervous tic that Orang Tua had noticed before. Now the elephant said, 'Will the truce hold, do you think?'

'If we turn on each other, we will just die a little bit sooner than if we wait for Man to kill us. This is our last chance.'

'Is it really a chance?'

Orang Tua did not answer.

Gajah said, 'Well, I'm ready to take on those puny humans!'

Orang Tua grinned, baring his long, yellow teeth. Gajah was a pygmy elephant. Smaller than the Indian elephant and much smaller than the massive African pachyderm with its ears like sails and tusks as thick as tree trunks.

Gajah was always ready for a fight to show that he was just as tough as his larger cousins.

Orang utan and elephant were distracted by the creature that stomped into the middle of the clearing. The animal bowed his head politely in their general direction. It was a very short-sighted beast. Orang Tua let the air whistle quietly through his teeth. Next to him, Gajah sucked in a deep breath, part awe and part relief.

Geram sensed the atmosphere change but did not know why. 'What is it? Who is this creature? I have never seen such a beast before.' Geram spoke in an excited whisper.

Orang Tua did not answer for a moment. He was at a loss for words.

At last, he said, his voice thick with emotion, 'That is the unicorn of Borneo.'

-eight-

The rhino with the distinct double horn was widely believed to be extinct in the wild. Despite that, rumours of sightings would occasionally filter through to the forest residents. Word would come that some animal had seen a hoof or a horn or a broad back deep in the rainforest. There would be general scepticism but also a tiny flicker of hope that maybe, just maybe, the unicorn of the rainforests had not disappeared from the earth.

One young orang utan, separated from his family group, was found days later, hungry, cold and gibbering about a massive horned beast he had seen deep in the forest. The clan, relieved to have him back and furious at him for having disappeared in the first place, was adamant he had imagined it. That had been almost fifty years ago and Orang Tua was an old beast now. And there, sparsely-haired, wrinkle-eyed, with one long horn and another shorter one, was the creature he had seen all those years ago. The two-horned rhino of Borneo – on the verge of extinction perhaps, but not quite there yet.

There was a fluttering in the leaves above them and a pearl grey, white-bellied sea-eagle settled on a low branch. She caught sight of the rhino and whistled.

'Goodness me! I thought you were extinct,' she squawked.

The rhino swivelled his large head and looked up towards the sound. 'Almost,' he said quietly. 'I am the last.'

The animals were silent. The magnitude of the doom facing them was brought sharply into focus.

'Then why are you here?' growled Harimau the tiger curiously, breaking the silence. 'It is too late for your species to be saved, whatever we do,' he continued bluntly.

Geram, though not the most sensitive of creatures, winced.

The rhino said firmly, 'Revenge.'

Orang Tua said, 'Well, talk of revenge may be premature. But today we have taken the first step for the survival of all our species. The presence of the rhino is an inspiration and a warning. If we do not act, and act together – we have no future.'

'What do you propose we do?' asked the rhino.

Orang Tua had given a lot of thought to this and he had a scheme. But he knew that there would be objections when the others heard it. He said, 'I have made a plan. It is bold and the odds of failure are very high. But if it works, we have a chance of survival.'

'So what is the plan?' asked Helang the sea-eagle,

spreading her wings and showing off her impressive wingspan.

Geram smothered a smile. The others would have to get used to Orang Tua. It was early days to be getting impatient. But he underestimated the old orang utan. Perhaps because the time had come for action, Orang Tua was brutally honest and to the point.

'My plan is twofold. The first is to attack the humans destroying the rainforests. We cannot win against their firesticks but we can buy ourselves time.'

'Time for what?' hissed Ular the python.

'Time for us to locate the Seeds from the earliest days and re-forest Borneo and the other rainforests.'

'If that's a plan, then I'm a duck!' screeched Helang rudely.

'We have old wives' tales of such Seeds,' grumbled Harimau the tiger dismissively. 'But there is no proof of such a thing. How would we find them anyway?'

Orang Tua asked, 'Do all of you have stories and folklore of such Seeds?'

There were nods and growls of assent from the animals.

Ular uncoiled himself and Geram prudently moved a couple of feet further away from the snake. Ular said, 'Like the orang utans, we too have a Collective Memory of ssssuch Seeds. But I do not know where they are.'

'If we all have knowledge of these Seeds, I think they must exist. As to where, I do not know. But I have a vision of a cold and white place where the wind cuts like a knife and the sun hides its face.'

Orang Tua's description was met with silence.

But then Ular the python nodded his great head. 'Yes*sss*, I too have seen such a place with my mind's eye. But in my vision the sky is not black but filled with glorious colour. Sheets of it flood the sky. Twinkling and sparkling like the sun on dewdrops. More beautiful than a rainbow.'

'Tomfoolery!' roared the tiger so fiercely that the other animals jumped with fright. 'Why do we listen to this nonsense?' he asked the others. 'If there are such Seeds, which I doubt, we will never find them from these ridiculous descriptions. Waves of colour in the sky. Wind that cuts like a knife. These are fairy stories!'

'Now, now. Don't be so sure,' said Helang, hopping from foot to foot on a branch. 'We eagles cover much greater distances than the rest of you. We soar higher than the canopy. We see for miles in every direction with our keen eyesight …'

'Yes, yes!' said Harimau irritably. 'We know you fly far and wide. What have you seen?'

'Nothing like you describe …'

'What? Then why are you wasting our time?'

Harimau was being unreasonable. And an unreasonable tiger was a force to be reckoned with. Geram bared his teeth angrily. Gajah turned pale although he was standing his ground.

Helang, who had provoked this irritation, prudently hopped onto a higher branch.

The rhino stepped in. He said, 'We do not have the luxury of time to argue. If we quarrel amongst ourselves, Man wins. Let us hear what the eagle has to say.'

Helang obliged in a slightly subdued voice. 'I have not seen these wonders myself but other raptors and hawks who have come from afar have spoken of such things.'

'What sort of things?'

'Of a white cold blanket called snow that envelopes the land for half the rotation of the earth. Of snowflakes that fall like leaves from the sky. Of stones of ice that hurtle to the earth.'

'And of these waves of colour?' asked Geram excitedly.

Helang puffed up her feathers, 'No, of that I have heard nothing.'

'We will have to seek out those who travel further than us to find out more,' said Orang Tua.

There were nods all around.

Orang Tua said slowly, 'There is one more thing.'

The others looked at him expectantly.

'We will need human help.'

'I do not understand what you mean,' said Gajah, curling his trunk in disgust.

'I meant exactly what I said. We will need *human* help to recover the Seeds.'

'Why do you ssssay ssssuch a ssssstupid thing?' hissed Ular the python, his accent getting stronger in his disbelief.

'What do they offer to us? Why would they help? What do they have that I don't?' growled Harimau.

'You mean, aside from opposable thumbs?' asked Orang Tua irritably.

Gajah snorted through his long trunk with sudden amusement. He asked, 'Seriously, Orang Tua. Why would we want human help? Aren't they the problem?'

'Are you imagining that we will wander around the world ourselves? Travel to a cold place? We will have to find the Seeds in the world of Man. We will not be able to do it without the help of men.'

'But why would they help us*ssss*?'

Orang Tua rubbed his eyes tiredly at the question from Ular.

'I do not believe that all humans are bad. We know that some work to protect animals …'

'Yes, in zoos!' interrupted Harimau.

'I am not saying they know what they are doing – just that a few of them understand that we have a right to exist too.'

'Even if you are right, Orang Tua, and some of the people are creatures of goodwill, how will we know which ones they are? How will we find them?' It was a sensible question from Geram.

It was the rhino that came to Orang Tua's rescue. He said in his slow, thoughtful way, 'I have heard that there are people who can understand animal speech. A few in every generation, Animal Talkers we call them. My own grandfather used to tell of a man who lived in Borneo who could understand the rhino.'

'What happened to him? Can we ask him?' Geram's excitement was palpable.

The rhino laughed. 'The span of human years is not long. This man has long since been the food of maggots. However, he worked hard to hide us from those who wanted our horns for medicine. The rhino thought highly of him.'

He paused for a moment, 'He would have been disappointed that his efforts were in vain. But if we could find one like him – I know such a human would agree to help us.'

Orang Tua said, 'I too have heard of the Animal Talkers. In fact, I believe that *all* humans were once Animal Talkers but they have lost the skill over the generations.'

The snake hissed in agreement. 'Yes*ss*, we have folk tales of a serpent who spoke to the earliest man and woman – and was later blamed when things began to go wrong – as if human greed was not enough to lead to their downfall!'

'There was once an Animal Talker who rescued the beasts, two by two, from a terrible flood,' continued Orang Tua.

'We are wasting our time. These Animal Talkers, if they existed at all, are as extinct as we are all going to be. We need to stop talking about humans who might help us and start fighting them instead,' snarled Harimau.

Helang swooped down to the middle of the clearing

from her perch. She said diffidently, 'I guess there is no harm keeping an eye out for an Animal Talker while looking for the Seeds.'

Orang Tua avoided the eye of the tiger. He said, 'That's a good idea.'

-nine-

He usually waited until he had closed a deal to light a celebratory Cuban cigar. But today, as Elliot Valentine stood on the porch of his ranch, he was so confident of the outcome that he lit up. He chewed on the end with his small, sharp teeth and exhaled a puff of grey smoke. It lingered above his head like a small cloud.

His valet came out and said deferentially, 'Everything is ready for the guests, sir.'

'I should think so. That's what I pay you for.'

'Yes sir.'

'We will go shooting tomorrow morning at dawn. Tell the men to chase some deer onto my land.'

'It is already done, sir.'

'And arrange for a barbecue. We will cook whatever we shoot.'

The wolf yelped and put a paw on Valentine's knee. A few seconds later, the sound of spitting gravel, picked up first by the wolf's sharp ears, was audible to Valentine as well. A car had arrived.

• • •

Father and son were not on speaking terms by the time they reached their destination. As they got out of the car, Dad said through clenched teeth, 'You just behave!' and then they crunched through the gravel to the man standing on the veranda with a cigar.

Elliot Valentine was very friendly. His face was wreathed in a welcoming smile. He clapped Spencer on the back and remarked that he was a fine-looking boy who would make any father proud. Spencer, sensing the tension in his Dad, terrified that his son would blow 'his big chance', managed to stutter a 'Th…thank you, Mr. Valentine.'

Dad was just awful. Spencer was ashamed of him and that feeling hurt more than anything else up to that moment. He sipped a freshly squeezed orange juice and heard his father agree that it was perfect hunting weather, that every man ought to pit his wits against that of an animal, that he had never understood people who objected to hunting on principle and that he himself was looking forward to an opportunity to 'bag a few' the following day.

Emboldened by this welcome from his potential employer, Richard asked if anyone else would be joining their weekend party. He had been worrying all the way that there would be other candidates and, as usual, he would be passed over for the job that he wanted so badly.

Valentine chuckled and his flesh trembled and Spencer's skin crawled. He said, 'Yes, I have a few business associates coming down whom I'd like you to meet.'

'Any other candidates for the job you have on offer?'

Spencer could tell Dad was trying to sound casual. But the slight tremor in his voice gave him away. Dad reminded him of a kid on his first day of school, scared of everything and everyone and desperate to make friends with someone so as not to be so alone.

'No, no!' Valentine chuckled. 'You're on a short list of one.'

His Dad's face broke out into a smile as wide as any Spencer had seen in years. 'Well,' he said, 'that is good news!'

-ten-

'Four score and seven years ago, our forefathers brought forth a new nation conceived in liberty and dedicated to the proposition that all men are created equal … ,' muttered Honesty under her breath, reciting the Gettysburg Address in an attempt to control her temper which was flaring red hot.

Honesty had been dropped at school by her Dad that morning. He had errands to run in town. Honesty had known exactly what would happen if her school mates saw the car with the sawn-off roof stinking of cow dung. She had asked her father to stop at the bottom of the street to avoid being spotted. She jumped out quickly and watched the car vanish down the street, backfiring all the way, confident that she hadn't been seen. But when she turned towards the school, Honesty saw Caitlin staring at her in open-mouthed wonder from across the road.

Honesty couldn't believe her bad luck. Why did it have to be Caitlin? Caitlin was a pretty, bubbly, blonde girl with suspiciously pink lips (make-up was banned at school). She was tiny and wore only shades of pink. Pink socks, pink blouse, short pink skirt, pink sneakers, pink blazer and a pink scrunchie holding back her hair. She looked like a young Barbie doll. In the deepest, most secret part of her heart, Honesty wanted more than anything else in the world to *be* Caitlin. Failing that, she wanted to be Caitlin's friend.

Unfortunately, Caitlin loved to pick on Honesty. She could be quite funny about hemp-wearing, organic vegetarians who believed they could talk to animals. And Caitlin always made sure that she had an audience. Usually it was a gang of eleven year old buffoons who modelled their behaviour after TV gangsters and followed Caitlin around like dogs on a lead.

The two girls walked to school on opposite sides of the street. Honesty kept her eyes firmly on the pavement. For one wild moment, she wondered whether to beg Caitlin to keep quiet about the car. But she knew there was no hope of convincing her. She had nothing to offer in return. She was most useful to Caitlin as a butt for her jokes.

The kids greeted the description of the stinking car with the tent roof with a combination of awe and merriment.

One of the boys asked her in genuine curiosity, 'But what makes it smell, Honesty?'

'Cow poo,' she said defiantly.

'What?'

'Cow poo!'

'But why would your parents do that?' asked Caitlin, forgetting to be funny for a moment.

'To avoid petroleum products,' said Honesty clearly. 'And reduce global warming. We use cow poo instead of petrol.'

There was a stunned silence and then a new outbreak of mirth.

Honesty recited the Gettysburg Address to herself. At this rate, she thought, she would need a longer speech.

Caitlin tossed her head and, Honesty noticed enviously, her blonde locks caught the sun and shone like fine gold. 'I'm not worried about global warming. If it gets a bit hotter around here, I'll just have to stop skiing and start surfing during the hols!' There were shouts of appreciation from the fan club.

'You could join me, Honesty. But I don't think they make hemp swimsuits!'

• • •

'I don't sssee how we are going to find a human who understands animals even if sssuch a person exists,' hissed Ular.

Harimau growled, a rumbling sound deep in his chest but did not say anything.

'And why should it be easier to hunt for an Animal Talker than the Seeds in the first place?' asked the rhino.

Helang stretched her wings and flapped them twice. She was getting stiff from standing still. She said thoughtfully, 'I am not sure about that. Such a person would be a curiosity amongst the animals. There's bound to be gossip about an Animal Talker.'

Gajah saluted Helang with his trunk. 'You are right, Helang. If we ask around, some creature somewhere would have heard of such a person.'

'Ask around?' purred Harimau sarcastically. 'What are you expecting us to do? Speak to every rodent? Question our prey before we devour them? Perhaps you would like me to gossip with the butterflies?'

Orang Tua laughed. 'You paint a vivid picture, Harimau. I have no objection to your doing any of those things. But perhaps the creatures best equipped for this job, as she suggests, are Helang and the higher birds.'

'Yes,' squawked Helang, 'except an Animal Talker might not have caught the attention of the eagles circling high in the sky.'

'That is true. But perhaps you could carry word to the land creatures of other continents?' asked Orang Tua.

Helang screeched. 'We can do that.'

'The creatures of the sea might be useful too?' This was a good suggestion from Gajah.

Helang said, 'I will speak to the whales. There is no point approaching the others. They have memories like goldfish!'

'What about the sharks?' rumbled Harimau.

'Would you trust a shark?' asked Gajah. 'High-end predators cannot control their instincts. We don't want to find an Animal Talker only to have it eaten!'

Harimau rose to his feet angrily and padded over to the elephant. 'What are you trying to say?' he growled.

'Only that you are such a highly-developed predator that, um…, you might get bored with such mundane tasks as being a messenger,' said Gajah, hastily retreating until he came up short against a tree trunk.

Harimau pondered the response for a moment, decided he was satisfied, lay down on the ground and started to lick his front paws.

Orang Tua was of the view they had pushed their luck far enough. He said authoritatively, 'Helang, will you spread the word?'

Helang nodded once, spread her huge wings, flew one tight circle around the clearing and then took to the skies. She was soon lost from view.

He turned to the rhino, 'You wish to spearhead the fighting?'

The last rhino inclined his great head.

'You realise that we are not trying to win a war against humans? We just need time for the search for the Seeds to be successful.'

The rhino swivelled his round ears forward thoughtfully – and then nodded again.

'Very well, we will meet back here in one week to discuss a plan of attack.'

There were grunts and growls of agreement.

The animals left the clearing one by one and soon only the rhino and the stench of death from the Rafflesia remained.

The rhino stood quietly, contemplating the enormity of the challenge. Then he lumbered over to the giant, stinking flower and ate it. He had no patience with bad omens.

● ● ●

His father shook him gently on the shoulder. At first, Spencer couldn't remember where he was. He buried his head in the pillow and murmured that he didn't feel like going to school. Then something about the bedding, the firmness of the mattress or the freshness of the bed sheets, brought the memories flooding back. He sat bolt upright and looked intently at his father and then out of the window where the darkness was blushing pink. Dawn was breaking.

'It's time to get up, son,' said Dad.

Spencer thought about refusing. But he didn't dare. His Dad was looking apologetic. Like he knew he was making Spencer unhappy and felt bad about it. But not bad enough to change his mind. Mum would never forgive him either if he ruined this chance for Dad. He knew his parents were tired of their New York lives. They were worried about him too. Spencer attended a school with metal detectors at the entrances, drug pushers in the canteen and graffiti on the toilet walls. Mum and Dad feared that he might join a gang or start taking drugs.

As it happened, it *was* a mean school. The teachers' first priority was to get transferred to another school. The big boys bullied the little ones. It was un-cool to be interested in lessons. But Spencer had learnt to look out for himself. He had quickly developed a reputation as a fighter, someone not to be pushed around. He was small but quick and tough. Spencer had never told Mum and Dad because they wouldn't understand. If he had not fought off some of the bullies, he would have needed protection from some other kid – and protection always came at a price.

Spencer turned over, rubbed his eyes and looked at his father.

He said, 'This is a mistake, Dad.'

Dad shook his head.

Spencer got out of bed.

Ten minutes later he was standing on the gravel driveway looking at the men who were prepared to wake up so early in the morning to shoot deer. There was Mr. Valentine in a large camouflage jacket, holding a gun, with his small feet tucked into high boots. Spencer was reminded of Puss-in-Boots and smothered a giggle with a cough.

There were two men other than his Dad and Mr. Valentine. Both were dressed in well-worn camouflage outfits, but there the resemblance ended. One man was rough, the other smooth. The smooth one was tall and very handsome in a plastic doll kind of way. He had wraparound sunglasses, grey temples in blonde hair and strong hands with long fingers. He made such a contrast to Mr. Valentine that the fat man looked like a reflection in a trick mirror.

The other stranger was crinkled – like a crushed up piece of paper that had been smoothed out. His face was thin and lined, with fine grooves fanning out from his eyes, two deep gouges running from his nose to his mouth and a tracing of veins like a spider's web over his cheeks. He had a vicious-looking scar, like a fat centipede, running from his forehead right down to his left eye. It caused his eye to droop. Spencer felt very jumpy. He kept expecting this miserable man to wink at him.

His Dad was introduced to the two men by Mr. Valentine. Mr. Smooth (Spencer had not caught their names) shook his father's hand firmly, smiled with big, white, even teeth and said, 'Good morning, Dr. Jones.' Mr. Rough grunted and looked away.

Dad had opted against buying himself camouflage. Mum was convinced that shiny new hunting clothes would make him look ridiculous. Valentine passed him a gun and Dad handled it as he would have done a venomous snake.

'Well now, Richard,' said Valentine, 'That there you're holding is a Browning rifle. Semi-automatic, pistol grip, short, even, single-stage pull. You point it at a buck and shoot. And we'll have venison for dinner tonight!'

Mr. Valentine turned his attention to Spencer. 'You must be very excited, young man. There's nothing quite like your first kill.'

Spencer hoped he did not look as petrified as he felt. Vain hope.

Mr. Smooth said understandingly, 'A bit nervous?

Nothing to worry about. You'll soon find your feet.'

Spencer gave him a sickly smile.

Mr. Valentine said, 'Well, let's get going!'

The men had started towards the Humvee when Valentine put up his hand in a signal to stop.

'We almost forgot something,' he chuckled gleefully.

He walked back to the house and reappeared carrying another rifle built on a smaller scale to the rest.

'Here's one for you, young man,' he said and held out the gun to Spencer.

Spencer saw Dad's pleading face over Valentine's shoulder and accepted the weapon. He didn't have to use it, he thought. The metal was cold in his hand and the barrel smooth. It felt dangerous.

Valentine said cheerfully, 'That gun was specially made for me on my tenth birthday. I killed my first deer that same afternoon. Maybe it will bring you the same luck, boy.'

-eleven-

Honesty was completely and utterly fed up. She was sick and tired of being different, of wearing weird clothes, of coming to school in a comedy car, of eating dull, disgusting food, of helping out with the chores on the farm and of having to sell stuff at the farmers' market. She had to do something about it. School had become unbearable since Caitlin had been downwind of the family car. She couldn't tell her parents. They would be shocked and uncomprehending. But she had to find a way to be less of a freak.

Honesty couldn't decide what she wanted most. Was it to have a Big Mac and fries? Was it to slump in front of a TV (forget plasma screens or LCD displays – she would settle for an old black and white) and watch something really, *really* mind-numbingly stupid? Did she want to wake up late and refuse to do any chores on the farm? Did she want to be dropped at school in a swanky new 4x4 Chelsea tractor by a Dad in a sharp suit (rather than in a turd mobile with a Dad in matching hemp overalls)? Did she more than anything else in the whole wide world want to wear pink, pink, PINK?

It was impossible to choose. Her mouth watered at the thought of the Big Mac but her heart leapt when she imagined herself in pink. Her brain loved the idea of putting down a book and watching telly. But her pride swelled at the thought of the big car and stylish father.

Honesty knew she was being ridiculous. There were much bigger problems in the world than her misery at school. There were floods, hurricanes and droughts. Only that morning, Mum had told her that the Baiji dolphin that had once lived in the Yangtze River in China was extinct. There were children all over the world who had a lot more to worry about than not having a television. There were nasty wars going on in faraway places. She heard enough about it at the dinner table as they ate their Fairtrade bananas and drank their Fairtrade hot chocolate. But Honesty was not in the mood to be sensible. She wanted to be a pink-wearing, TV-watching, junk food-eating, *popular* child and she was not going to be happy otherwise.

Honesty snuck out the back door into the garden. She made her way on all fours along the other side of the wall so her mother wouldn't see her go. She scrambled up her favourite tree in the middle of the apple orchard and annoyed the cat who was already there. Honesty didn't care. She needed to think.

• • •

Catching an updraft, Helang, the sea-eagle, climbed higher. From the ground she looked like a small smudge in the deep blue sky. The air was thin here but she was riding the winds and not using much energy. The lack of oxygen did not bother her. Helang was on the second part of her mission.

The first part had been easy. She had, with loud, squawking calls, summoned the eagles. They had come from far and wide – all curious to see if Helang had survived her encounter with tigers and pythons. The birds had swooped down to the tallest tree in Borneo, an emergent so high that its leaves were often hidden by billowing white clouds. They perched in rows, like pigeons on a telephone wire, waiting to hear what Helang had to say. Helang explained the need to seek out an Animal Talker – a human who could communicate with animals. The sea-eagles were sceptical about the idea – unwilling to believe that any of the creatures they saw slashing and burning their way through the rainforests would be willing to help. But Helang had reminded them of Animal Talkers throughout history who had been of assistance to the beasts – including one, St. Francis, whom even the humans thought of as a saint. In the end they had agreed to carry out the wishes of the Council of Beasts.

Helang had also urged them to cross-examine all the Higher Beasts they came across to see if they had any hints in their Collective Memory about where the Seeds might be. She had explained the combined understanding of the

Council so far – of a place covered in blankets of snow with waves of colour in the sky. This task had appealed to them and the eagles had taken off from the tree like fighter jets from an aircraft carrier.

Now Helang was looking for whales. It was extremely important that the creatures of the ocean take part in the quest to find the Animal Talker – and the Seeds. Land creatures were landlocked, unable to travel freely and far. But she and her kind could cleave through the air as long as their wings had strength. The whales traversed even greater distances – entire oceans were their playing and feeding grounds.

She looked for the telltale spray of water to burst into the air like fireworks. She would know she had found her whales when she saw that. But so far she had not spotted a single whale and she was feeling hungry. Perhaps it was time to fly a bit lower and look for slivers of silver under the water instead. She felt like fish for lunch.

Helang descended, gliding downwards in lazy circles, her eyes peeled for whales and, failing that, lunch. She saw a fleet of fishing trawlers in the distance and screeched in irritation. Helang flew closer and saw the V-shaped white trails in the waves behind each boat. The nets these boats used were so huge and wide that they could empty an entire stretch of ocean, leaving passing sea-eagles hungry and tired. In the past, she had managed to steal fish, recently caught and still thrashing about, from the deck of a trawler. Perhaps she could try that again, although it was a risky strategy.

Helang pulled out of her dive and hovered above the boat. She was not going to land on board to steal fish without knowing exactly what she was up against. To her disappointment, there was not a single fish on the deck. Helang climbed higher again, her stomach tight with hunger. She saw a plume of water burst forth in the distance catching the light and reflecting all the colours of the rainbow.

Whales!

• • •

After a brief and inadequate explanation of how guns worked, to which Spencer listened mutely, he certainly didn't plan to shoot anything, while Dad pretended to nod in understanding, they made their way in single file through the forest. In the lead was Mr. Smooth, looking very natural as he found the best way through clusters of hardwoods and conifers. Tiptoeing after him, and combining menace with comedy, his new camouflage jacket shining greener than the trees, was Mr. Valentine.

Dad was next. He followed as quietly as he could but he kept stepping on broken twigs and dry, crackling leaves. Spencer trailed after him, nervous, but light on his feet. If it wasn't for the fact that the aim was to shoot something at the end of it, he would really have enjoyed this trek through the wilderness. It was so different from New York City.

Mr. Rough brought up the rear. Spencer could hear him muttering under his breath although no words were audible. He would not have been surprised to be shot in the back.

Mr. Smooth waved them all to a standstill. He whispered, 'We should fan out. See whether we can spot any deer. Remember, whitey likes trees for cover and brushy growth for food.'

Spencer had no idea what he was talking about until he realised that 'whitey' must be a nickname for the white-tailed deer. These people had a cuddly nickname for something they were planning to blow away with a semi-automatic rifle. What did they put in the water in these parts?

Mr. Smooth continued, 'There are a few shooting platforms in the trees if someone wants to try for a high shot.'

He waved his hand in an arc to indicate the direction they were to go. Dad signalled to Spencer to stay near him but Spencer pretended not to understand. He set off purposefully and alone. If by some chance he came across a deer first, he might be able to chase it away. Whatever happened, there was no way he planned to shoot anything, except perhaps Mr. Valentine. Spencer shuddered. He did not like the fat man with his missing finger. Spencer was sure Valentine would have been the sort of kid who pulled the wings off butterflies. He had probably dissected frogs with the kitchen knife too. He just could not understand why Dad was sucking up to this guy. So what if there was a good job on offer? There were bound to be others.

Spencer walked quietly into the woods. He wished he knew what sort of trees these were. He was sure he recognised the maple tree from the pointy leaves but what were the others? It crossed his mind that if he was not careful, he might get lost. This was becoming like something out of Hansel and Gretel. He half expected to turn a corner and find a gingerbread house. Spencer felt in his pockets for something to leave a trail with. There was nothing useful. A piece of string too short to tie to a tree and use as a guide. One smooth black stone that he had collected some time back in Central Park because of the swirly patterns on its surface and a sweet that he immediately popped in his mouth.

There was nothing for it. No city boy should get lost in the forest, he decided. Not when the city boy in question had no survival skills. He tried to imagine how he might start a fire to keep warm by rubbing two sticks together. Or he might weave a little shelter for himself from leaves and vines. Spencer grinned. He certainly hoped it wouldn't come to that. He made up his mind to stay put and found a flat rock under a tree with a silvery trunk, delicate light branches and fluttering leaves.

He leaned his gun carefully against the trunk and sat down. Spencer stretched his legs and concluded that the whole episode might not turn out that badly after all. He had imagined they would spend the morning potting deer after deer until he was wallowing in slippery red blood. But so far there was no sign of wildlife at all, not even rabbits or squirrels or wild turkeys. With luck the others would soon get bored with their deer hunt. They would head back to the ranch and he and Dad would leave this hateful place and never come back.

'I would hate to shoot a deer,' Spencer said sleepily to himself.

'I should think not, a young thing like you!' whispered a soft voice.

Startled, Spencer leapt to his feet and grabbed the gun. He looked around, wondering who had spoken. Was it one of the men?

There was no one to be seen and he shook his head wondering if he had dozed off under the tree and dreamt the remark.

'I'm over here,' said the voice again. Spencer whirled around and came face to face with a young buck. The creature was beautiful, with nut brown fur and liquid eyes. The antlers on his head were just two small forked prongs.

Spencer was flabbergasted. He could not believe his ears. Had the deer spoken to him?

'Why are you so surprised?' asked the buck. 'Haven't you ever spoken to an animal before?'

Spencer shook his head mutely. A small part of his mind realised that the deer was not using human speech. It was just that he understood the gentle bleating in human terms.

The rest of his brain was just gibbering with shock.

'But, but ...' he trailed off. His first chance ever to speak to an animal and he was going to blow it. He mentally grabbed himself by the shoulders, gave himself a good shake and tried again. 'But, but ... how?'

The creature took pity of him. 'I don't know how. Once, all humans were Animal Talkers. Now there are hardly any left. When I saw you under the tree, I thought you might be one.'

'Why?'

The deer shrugged delicately, 'Instinct, I guess. I *am* an animal, after all.'

Spencer was perplexed. 'But what about dogs and cats and stuff? Why haven't I ever understood them?'

'Are those the *slave* animals?'

'Well, we call them pets ...'

'You probably weren't listening. You have to start young, really concentrate hard ... or not concentrate at all, to understand animal speech.'

Spencer filed the information away for further consideration later.

'The creatures have been on the lookout for an Animal Talker,' the buck continued.

'What's an Animal Talker?'

'Someone like you.'

'Awesome! Err ... why?'

The deer did not reply. He said instead, 'Why do you have that firestick?'

Spencer did not understand what the creature was talking about and then realised he was holding the gun. He flung it away in disgust and it landed between them. The deer skittered back a few feet.

Spencer said, 'No, don't be afraid. I'm sorry! I would never hurt you.'

'Firesticks have killed many of my kind.'

Spencer hung his head in shame. What could he say? Even as he stood there his own Dad was out in the forest somewhere trying to kill a deer. Dad, the others!

He said urgently to the deer, 'You must get away. There are others trying to hunt you!'

The deer looked around nervously, lifting its tail and showing the white streak on its underside that gave it its name. 'Are you sure? Where?'

Spencer said, panic stricken. 'I don't know. We fanned out. They could be anywhere!'

Even as he spoke there was the loud crack of a rifle. Spencer thought at first the shot had missed or been aimed elsewhere. Then the buck sank to his knees. Blood welled up from a bullet wound on the animal's side. The red was already matting the glossy fur. The deer raised his head slightly and kicked feebly with his spindly, elegant legs, trying to get enough purchase on the ground to get up. It was no use. He lay back down on the leafy forest floor.

Spencer sank to his knees beside the young buck. 'Try and get up,' he begged. 'I will hide you. I can distract them while you get away …'

The deer's eyes were filled with pain. It whispered, 'It's too late. But … I do not want to die by a hunter's bullet. Can you help me?'

'How?' asked Spencer.

He followed the deer's gaze. It was looking at his gun.

He shook his head.

The deer said, 'Please.'

Spencer got up and grabbed the rifle. He cocked it and pointed it at the deer. His hands were shaking and he could barely see through the tears in his eyes.

The buck spoke, its voice breathy and tired, 'You must do this to help me.'

In the distance and coming nearer, Spencer could hear the sounds of the others crashing through the undergrowth.

He raised the gun.

'What is your name?' the wild creature asked.

'Spencer.'

'I am Achak.'

Spencer shot the deer in the head and watched the light in its eyes flicker and go out like a candle in a sudden gust.

Then he dropped the gun and curled up on the ground. They found him a few seconds later. Dad picked him up. Spencer was rigid in his arms, his pupils wide with shock.

The other men were very impressed that Spencer had had the presence of mind to ensure the kill with a second shot.

'Not that it could have escaped with that wound,' said

Mr. Smooth. 'It was a good shot of yours, Elliot.'

'It was too easy. The creature was just standing there.'

Mr. Rough efficiently chopped a sapling, stripped it of leaves and tied the deer's ankles to it. He hoisted one end on a shoulder and Mr. Smooth grabbed the other.

They made a slow procession back to the vehicle. Successful hunters with their trophy. And a boy who had spoken to a deer and shot it the same morning.

-twelve-

The day Spencer shot the deer, Honesty stole money from her Mum. She waited for her to go out into the garden. Then she opened the drawer where Mum kept her large purse (woven by a women's cooperative in Guatemala) and extracted a fistful of notes. Honesty was fairly sure her mother would not notice anything missing. Mum's accounting method (it drove Dad nuts) was to simply stuff whatever she needed – money, receipts and bills – higgledy-piggledy into her purse on the basis that at least she knew where everything was if ever she really needed it.

Honesty hurried to her room, locked the door and peered out of the window from behind the curtains. Mum was weeding the asparagus industriously. She would be there for a while. Honesty sat on the homemade patchwork quilt on the bed and counted the money she had nicked. Sixty pounds! She was rich.

• • •

It was not difficult to rally the orang utans. The call went out far and wide in the jungles of Borneo. Young males and females with no children came forward without hesitation. They knew that they could not match the might of Man. But if death was a certainty and extinction imminent, why not choose the moment and manner of death rather than wait for the fires and be consumed? Orang Tua and Geram returned to the clearing deep in the forest with fifty beasts.

Harimau brought twenty tigers. It was a huge achievement. Tigers were loners. To have roused twenty of them to fight demonstrated the influence the cantankerous old creature had over his kind. It also showed the desperation that had taken hold of even this most feared predator. Driven to seek food from the livestock of humans by ever shrinking hunting grounds, slinking around *kampungs* at night hoping to seize a cow or a goat, pursued deep into the jungle by angry, frightened villagers, shot for skin and bones by poachers – the tigers were ready to push back.

Helang had sent five birds under the command of a young male brahminy kite. Small, smart predators – they were to be the eyes and ears of the troops. Large numbers of birds were not needed. Helang and the rest of the eagles were best used looking for an Animal Talker or the Seeds. In fact, Orang Tua had suggested diffidently to the prickly sea-eagle that they might ask the hornbills instead of the kites. Helang had screeched with laughter. 'The hornbills?

They carry their brains in their horns!' As the horns of these unique birds were hollow, this was quite an insult. Orang Tua was glad that none of the large birds with their extravagant bills were within earshot of this remark.

Gajah brought fifty pygmy elephants. They were lined up in rows, five wide and ten deep. He was proud of their discipline compared to the lounging tigers and the excited, chattering orang utans.

The pythons had twirled themselves around one long overhanging branch of a *tembusu* tree that jutted out over the clearing. It was impossible to tell where one snake ended and another began. Coils overlapped and heads and tails were entwined. Only the occasional unblinking eye or flickering tongue distinguished one from another. Gajah wondered whether the extra weight of the uncountable pythons might bring the branch down. He ordered his troops twenty paces back. The rhino, standing silently in the middle of the clearing, caught Gajah's eye, glanced up and took a few stately paces to the left. As the last two-horned rhino of Borneo, he was looking forward to a hero's death. Not death by falling pythons.

The rhino said quietly but with authority, 'Are we all here?'

The animals recognised their cue. 'Fifty orang utans,' said Orang Tua respectfully.

'Twenty tigers,' growled Harimau proudly. 'More can be mustered, if we are lost in battle.'

'The reconnaissance wing is here, sir!' squawked the

brahminy kite whose name was Burung.

'We are here. There are twenty of usss,' hissed Ular from the branch above, raising his big head and looking down at the gathering. He added, 'I have brought reinforcementsss.'

The animals listened expectantly. But Ular did not speak. Instead he slithered down the tree and then into the jungle. The other creatures waited patiently, or impatiently, as their natures dictated. In a few minutes Ular was back, bringing with him seven King Cobras. There was a sharp intake of breath from Orang Tua. He had, at the outset, considered inviting the cobras. They were Higher Beasts too and their cunning was legendary. But so was their cruelty and selfishness and in the end he had decided their presence would not be an advantage. Now Ular had brought them. Orang Tua glanced at the rhino. He was in charge.

The rhino said, 'We are always pleased for more assistance in this battle. Are you willing to fight under my command?'

The lead cobra rose up and swayed gently, as if he alone could sense a gentle breeze in the still air. His hood flattened. The delicate diamond patterns on the back of his head were clearly visible to Gajah and his troops massed behind the snake. The two obsidian orbs that were the cobra's eyes looked directly into those of the rhino. The rhino did not flinch even though the snake's venom was powerful enough to kill him.

The cobra ducked suddenly and Orang Tua thought for

a horrible moment it was lunging at the rhino. His gasp died in his throat as it became apparent that the serpent was bowing its head. The king of the snakes said in a flat, thin, echo-less voice, 'We will work under your command.'

'Then you are welcome to join us.'

• • •

One of the sailors on lookout hollered and all the boats turned in the direction of the whales.

Helang could see the enormous mammals under the water. It was a pod of humpback whales – large, blackish-grey baleen whales with prominent humps and long flippers. They were swimming quickly but not as quickly as the motorised boats behind them. There was shouting and activity on the deck and a sailor on the first boat fired a harpoon. It snaked through the air attached to a long, thick wire tail. The harpoon plunged into the back of one of the whales who ploughed onwards, dragging the boat after it. Helang could hear the men yelling with exhilaration as they bore down on the great whale. The animal struggled in the water, weak with fatigue and blood loss. The thrashings of its huge tail were getting feeble.

The whalers reeled the great beast in. They tied a rope to its tail and started to winch it on board. The whale was gasping for air. The men on the deck were leaping about, shouting and high-fiving. They had landed a whale on their first attempt of the day. It was going to be a good expedition. They could sense it.

Helang flew after the other whales. After this, at least they should be willing to help.

• • •

'Well, the job's your's if you want it,' said Valentine. It was a contract to do surveys in Alaska with Texic, Valentine's oil company.

Spencer's Dad was too excited to speak. He just nodded.

'World oil prices are at an all time high. There's money to look for oil in places that were previously too expensive to tap. The melting glaciers are opening up new areas to be explored as well,' continued Valentine smugly.

'Sir, I'm convinced there are vast oil and gas reserves under the ice and snow of the Arctic Circle,' agreed Spencer's Dad.

Valentine stabbed a finger into his chest, 'I want you to find it for me and I want Texic to be the first to exploit it.'

Gone were the days when grizzled wildcatters on the plains of Texas would sink a hole in the ground and watch the oil gush out. Now, expertise was needed. Boffins like Spencer's Dad, who had a background in geology and specialised in Arctic conditions, had no idea of their own worth in this brave new world. Richard Jones did not look the part of an old-fashioned oilman who could sniff out black gold hundreds of metres beneath the earth. He was not tanned and unshaven. He did not drink or swear. He was thin, tall and his clothes hung on him. But he was the man Mr. Valentine needed.

Spencer had hardly uttered a word since shooting the deer. He walked beside the body of Achak and rode back to the ranch with it. He watched as they carried the buck around the back to be skinned and quartered in preparation for the barbecue. Then he went to his room, had a hot shower, climbed into bed and refused to get out again. His father told Valentine that he had caught a cold on the hunt.

Spencer only agreed to leave his room the next morning to get into the car. He huddled in the front seat with a couple of blankets and again Dad made his excuses. Valentine didn't care. He had what he wanted – someone to find oil under the Arctic ice.

• • •

Honesty played truant from school. She set off as usual, waving goodbye to her Mum. She felt a twinge of guilt but firmly suppressed it. When she got to town, she went straight to McDonald's, walked in under the golden arches and ordered a Big Mac with fries and a Coke.

She started with the fries. They were delicious. Crunchy, not soggy. Thin and long for convenience – not in the least potato shaped. And very salty. Honesty wondered how such long fries came from a potato in the first place. They must have really big potatoes on their farms, she decided. Perhaps it was the chemical fertilisers.

Next, Honesty sucked up a huge gulp of Coke – and started to splutter. Gas bubbles were going up her nose and exploding like small firecrackers. When she recovered from her bout of sneezing and coughing she looked around surreptitiously. Was it supposed to be like that or was her Coke off? Nobody else seemed to be having any trouble. She had a couple more small sips. Perhaps it was one of those things you had to get used to before you realised that you loved it.

Finally, it was the moment she'd been waiting for. Honesty felt all tingly with excitement. It was time to try the Big Mac. She opened the warm cardboard box. There were two beef patties in three layers of bun! She tried to pick it up and half the contents of the burger shot out the back and fell on the tray. Honesty ended up with a mouthful of limp salad leaves, a bit of bun and some processed cheese. Honesty decided she was quite full from the fries. The Coke had made her tummy feel funny. Maybe today was not the day for a Big Mac as well. You could have too much of a good thing. She didn't want to feel ill and give Mum an excuse to dose her with home-brewed tonics. And what if she chucked up the fries at home? That would be a nasty way to get found out. She had enough money to come back the next day. Besides, the shops were opening!

Honesty grabbed her school bag and headed for the nearest shop. It was a big department store. She stepped out of an elevator and her breath caught in her throat. It was paradise. The girls' clothes were amazing. Straps and skirts, pleats and pictures, buttons and sequins and pink, pink, pink everywhere. Hot pink, baby pink, fuchsia, rose, blush – any and every sort of pink that a girl could desire.

Honesty chose with trembling hands. She could hardly believe what she was doing. She fingered the soft cottons and silky satins and prudently checked the prices. Nothing was made of hemp and nothing seemed too expensive to a girl with sixty pounds in her bag. Honesty tried to ignore the voice in her head that sounded like Mum. Cheap prices were only possible if other Mums and Dads weren't paid enough for the work they did, the voice said. Maybe their kids didn't get enough food or didn't go to school. Or worse, maybe the kids were the ones working in the factories.

The shop was starting to fill up. All these people couldn't be wrong, could they, wondered Honesty? Surely they wouldn't buy the clothes if children were forced to sew them or the factories were pumping poison into the rivers? Mum was exaggerating. She did that sometimes.

Honesty took her carefully chosen pink wardrobe and walked to the checkout. She paid quietly, keeping her eyes on the floor, convinced someone was going to ask her why she was alone and where the money had come from. But nobody did. She walked out with her clothes neatly packed in a plastic bag. She ignored the same little voice in her head – it was getting easier to tune out – warning her of the fate of turtles that mistook the plastic bags for a jelly fish lunch.

Honesty heard one of the checkout women say to the other, 'Even carrot tops want to wear pink!' She had a moment of doubt. And then shrugged her skinny shoulders. So what if pink wasn't her best colour? She had the clothes she wanted.

Honesty hurried up the street in the direction of school. Two hundred yards from the gate was a public toilet. She changed quickly into her new clothes. She stuffed the old ones into the plastic bag and then into her school bag. She paused to regret that she had not thought to buy a new satchel. Tomorrow, perhaps. The mirrors in the toilets were cracked and stained. All she could see were shards of pink and slivers of a smiling face. Feeling happy but very, very self-conscious, Honesty hurried to school.

-thirteen-

The whales floated on the surface, sucking in huge breaths of air to replenish their oxygen-depleted bodies. They were exhausted. They had swum far and fast to escape the harpoons.

The humpback they had lost was a young female. It was tough for young whales to survive to adulthood. New mothers were weak from lack of food and could not wean the small ones. There were many desperate predators as food in the oceans grew scarce. Whales got entangled in deep sea nets – especially the babies who didn't know how to look out for man-made traps. To lose a healthy young female, who had overcome all the obstacles to reach maturity, was a bitter blow to the pod.

The whales listened to Helang the eagle in surly silence. They knew about the Council of Beasts meeting in the Borneo rainforest. There was not much the whales missed as they criss-crossed the oceans singing their laments. But humpback whales were fatalists. It was not their way to fight against the future. They, who had long navigated by the stars, would look to the heavens on an inky black night and nod and call to each other. The stars did not change. They were constant. The great constellations knew their place in the heavens and the whales knew their place beneath the seas. They would weep for fallen sisters but they would not act to thwart the will of Nature.

'But it is not Nature. It is Man!' Helang argued in exasperation.

A whale so old that his undersides were completely hidden by barnacles summed it up, 'Only when Orion himself comes down from the heavens and tells us to join your quest, will we do so.'

'But surely you have heard of these humans who can understand the animals?' asked Helang.

'Of course we have,' said the oldest humpback whale. 'In our history, stories are told of an Animal Talker named Ahab who fought a battle with our kind. He understood the song of the whales but he believed that he was insane. He swore to kill the legendary white whale, Moby Dick, who spoke to him, and destroy the very source of his madness. It was an epic battle. In the end, we believe that the sailor did go mad. That is what happens when humans understand us. To believe that they might help, to ask us to seek them out on the day that our young one has been harpooned … I believe you must have flown too close to the sun and it has singed your brain!'

• • •

Honesty was a hit. The kids loved the new look. Honesty hadn't known it when buying the clothes, but she had picked the Powder Pink Princess range that was all the rage. In fact, she had selected the latest version of the Powder Pink Princess Pullover that even Caitlin didn't have. The girls latched on to her. The boys could see which way the wind was blowing and stopped moo-ing.

Caitlin giggled and whispered to her that she'd kissed Johnny Perkins behind the gym and made her promise not to tell anyone in a tone that suggested that she meant the opposite. Nobody seemed to care that Honesty's clothes did not match her hair. The fact that Honesty had read a lot of books became something to be proud of – the girls were prepared to consider that it might be cool if you had the right clothes to go with it. And finally, Johnny Perkins had sidled up to her and suggested that they meet behind the gym. Her cup was full.

• • •

Spencer's Dad packed immediately. After a brief hesitation, his Mum decided they should all go with him to Alaska instead of waiting to see how the job turned out first. Spencer did not know it, but he was the main reason she opted to uproot the family and move. Spencer had been silent and morose since getting back from the hunting trip. He spoke in monosyllables and picked at his food. His teacher sent a note asking if everything was alright at home.

His mother knew that he had shot the deer. Spencer hadn't told her, but his father had. She understood that he might feel sadness. But she was unprepared for this deep depression.

Richard tried to reassure her. He was sure Spencer would snap out of it. It was just a phase. The buck was almost dead when Spencer shot it. Delighted about his new job but guilty at having dragged Spencer on the trip, Spencer's Dad was very keen to believe that his son's regret was just a minor matter that would soon clear itself up.

His mother shook her head in confusion. 'No, Richard. He isn't the same boy. He doesn't speak and he doesn't smile. He just sits in his room and I swear sometimes I see tears in his eyes.'

They both turned to the empty chair in the kitchen as if expecting to see the ghost of the old Spencer sitting there, munching his biscuits and babbling away about whatever came into his head.

Spencer's mother continued, 'He hasn't said a word about that trip since he got back. But killing an animal is something that could break the heart of a boy like Spencer. Do you know why he did it?'

'No.'

'I just can't see why he would have gone and killed a deer. But I can see why it might have hurt him too much for bearing.'

'What shall we do?' asked Richard.

'We'll all go to Alaska.'

Richard said in agreement, 'It might take Spencer's mind off things.'

A tear hovered at the corner of her eye, a bright jewel of sadness, 'I sure hope you're right. I can't bear to see him like this.'

'Me neither,' muttered Spencer's father.

• • •

Reports were coming in. A dog in Singapore was sure that someone had spoken to him once. Two cats in Paris swore that a stranger in a park had understood their comments about the state of French pavements. A sheep farm on the Falkland Islands sent word that one of the shepherd boys seemed to understand that sheep loved grazing on a hillside on a beautiful summer's day more than anything else in the world. But nothing was conclusive. Helang, who was collecting the information on potential Animal Talkers as it came in from the eagles who in turn had heard it from other eagles who had heard it from owls and egrets and even a surprisingly lucid mynah bird, was not convinced. Dogs were notoriously stupid even by the standards of domesticated animals. Cats were so mean-spirited that they could easily be lying just for the fun of it. As for the sheep from the Falklands, Helang knew that they loved grazing on a hillside in summer. She doubted it needed a shepherd boy who understood their baa-ing to work that out.

The sea-eagle sent word for the stories to be verified and regularly updated the rhino as to progress, or lack of it. But Helang did not believe that they had found their Animal Talker. It was early days yet though and she did not despair.

She had better luck with the Seeds. Gorillas from the boreal forests on Mt. Kilimanjaro sent word that there were tales of the Seeds in their folklore. No one had ever taken it seriously but, for what it was worth, they had a Collective Memory of white sheets over the ground. There was no mention of coloured skies. But there was a faded image of five fingers that beckoned the seekers of the Seeds through a gateway. And a clear memory of intense bone-chilling cold, quite outside anything the gorillas had ever experienced in the Congo. The gorillas had also sent word that, if there were any spare Seeds, they would love to have some. The deforestation situation was very bad where they were too. Gorilla numbers were dwindling and they did not expect to survive another generation.

Even better was the word that came from a large parched island where, the brahminy kite carrying the information told Helang, the winter was summer and the summer was winter. There were weird and ancient creatures there, Higher Beasts that did not occur anywhere else the bird had been. A hopping beast, with huge hind legs and small front paws, had told her that the Seeds were protected on a green mountain by sea-dwelling unicorns and snowy white bears. This had sounded more like a fable than a Collective

Memory. Still, it was the most detailed information Helang had received yet. It remained to be seen if it was sufficient for an Animal Talker to interpret.

• • •

Honesty fell into a routine. Every few days she would take some money from her mother's purse. She would buy herself a fast food snack on the way home from school. She did not dare stop on the way to school, as she had done on the first day, in case she got into trouble for arriving late.

She rented a locker at the bus station and kept her new clothes there – to change on the way to and from school. She added a few tasteful items to her new wardrobe – largely pink, of course. But she felt bold enough to buy herself some purple leggings. Caitlin was officially her best friend now. They went everywhere together and giggled a lot. Honesty felt that her influence was sufficient to start trying to be a leader and not just a follower. She was enjoying every minute of her new life. She asked the kids at school to call her Honey.

Her biggest remaining problem was that she did not know how to arrange to watch television regularly. She had found a temporary solution. If she spent half an hour every week studying the TV Guide in bed by torchlight, she could take part in conversations at school. Quite often it was enough to say things like, 'Did you see that on the telly last night?' and 'Like, how cool was that?'

In the evenings, Honesty did her chores as before. In fact, she did them more willingly than usual because she felt awful when she saw Mum's happy face as she got home from school every day. Honesty felt guilty – but not guilty enough to abandon her double life. Being popular was just too much fun. She couldn't give it up. Not yet. There was no way she would keep any of her new friends if she reverted to puke-coloured hemp clothes.

'Honesty!'

Honesty started and looked at her mother.

'You didn't eat your sandwich at school today. You must be famished.'

Honesty gave herself a mental kicking. She had forgotten to throw away her sandwich. She must not get careless. That was the surest way to discovery. She had enjoyed munching on her Whopper with cheese all the way home. And she had remembered to fold the greaseproof paper into a small pellet and shove it into the middle of a thick hedge before she reached the house. But she had forgotten to feed her packed lunch to a passing sheep.

Mum held up the vegetable sandwich (organic rye bread baked at home) and looked at Honesty worriedly.

'Do you want me to make you something hot, Honey?'

Honesty shook her head hurriedly. 'No, Mum. I just wasn't hungry today.'

Mum looked even more concerned and the sharp horizontal frown line that she saved for serious occasions appeared on her forehead. 'You must be coming down with something, darling. I'll give you a good dose of my special berry tonic.'

Honesty submitted to a spoonful of the disgusting concoction with good grace. It was a lesson, she thought, not to get complacent.

• • •

The rhino sent brahminy kites out on reconnaissance missions to all the major sites of human activity in Borneo. He needed to know as much as possible before he committed troops to action. As to the general approach, he was briefing Orang Tua and the other species leaders.

'We don't want the humans to know there is a war on,' he said. 'Not yet anyway.'

'Why not?' demanded Harimau.

'Because if they suspect anything, they will raze the rainforests to the ground and hunt every single one of us to extinction,' snapped the rhino.

Harimau subsided and the rhino went on, 'There are two groups we need to target – the humans clearing the land for plantations and the loggers. When the kites report back we will know which camps to focus on.'

'How will we target them if we aren't going to attack them?' asked Ular.

'We are! But we are not going to take them head on. We are going to work on sabotaging their efforts, not killing ourselves.'

The brahminy kites reported back quickly. The rhino listened impassively to the details of Man methodically destroying the jungles of Borneo. The animals knew it was happening. That was why the cornered beasts had decided to fight back. But even the rhino, last of his kind, was surprised by the scale of the rainforest destruction. They had their work cut out for them if they were going to buy enough time to find the Seeds and preserve the forests.

The rhino was sceptical about the ancient tale of the Seeds. Even if they did exist, he did not hold out much hope of finding them. But the last rhino did not particularly care. Whatever happened, it was too late for him and his species. He just wanted some payback.

He said, 'There are not many of us but humans multiply like maggots on a carcass. We must find their weaknesses and strike quickly, quietly and hard.'

There were grunts and growls of agreement. This was the sort of war talk they wanted to hear.

'I have picked a camp of humans clearing the forest for oil palm plantations.'

'Why only one?' asked Orang Tua. 'There must be hundreds of them.'

'I should have said, one first, as an experiment – then five at a time. We don't have the beastpower for more. And I want a chance to adjust tactics if I have to.'

'So what do we do?' asked Orang Tua.

'I am dividing us into groups with representation from each of the species here.'

There were surprised and angry mutters. All the creatures had assumed they would work with their own kind. They had expected to coordinate their actions of course – but to work in multi-species groups – that was controversial.

The rhino had anticipated this.

'We will need *all* our unique skills in each group,' he said patiently.

Geram voiced the thoughts of the group. 'Can we trust each other?' he asked, looking around at the predators that surrounded him, their eyes glinting in the half darkness.

'We're going to have to,' said the rhino grimly.

• • •

Kai was fuming. He had watched his sister, whom he loved dearly, be harpooned in the name of scientific research. He had listened to Helang's impassioned plea for help while his own salty tears were carried away on the ocean currents. He had kept silent as the old humpback had spoken of the wisdom written in the stars. He had bitten his tongue as his elders had invoked the name of Ahab to explain their disdain for the plan to find the first Seeds with the help of an Animal Talker. He had watched as Helang had flown away in disgust at her failed mission.

Then Kai turned to the old whale and said, 'My sister is dead. How are you so sure that you are right?'

The old whale fluted his sadness to lose one so precious to the pod but did not back down.

'Our wisdom is that of generations. We are guided by the unchanging stars. We do not make short-term decisions where the consequences are unknown.'

Kai had gotten angrier and angrier. 'We know the short-term *and* long-term consequences of doing nothing,' he shouted, unmelodic in his anger. 'More will die at the point of a harpoon. The rest of us will linger and eventually succumb to starvation. The oceans will fall silent as the song of the humpbacks is no more! Surely we should help those who are fighting the domination of Man?'

There was a keening from all the whales as he said this. Kai waited, hoping someone would step in on his side and plead that they do something, anything, rather than just swim away from their troubles. But he waited in vain. None of the others dared to defy the old whale.

With a despairing cry that resonated through the seas, Kai turned his back on the pod and, using his huge tail to propel him strongly through the water, left his fellow whales to their fate. He had decided. He would not swim by and do nothing. Kai did not know how he could possibly contribute to the fight – but he was going to try. The stars might be prepared to witness every single whale go the way of his beloved sister, but Kai was not.

-fourteen-

The day began like any other Sunday. Honesty and her Mum packed for the farmers' market. They crammed boxes of fruit and vegetables into the back of the car. Honesty dressed quickly, much less annoyed by her scratchy hemp clothes than normal. After all, she hadn't worn them much that week.

The first sign of trouble came when Mum grabbed her purse. She usually left it on the table by the door so that she would catch a glimpse of it on her way out. Otherwise, she inevitably forgot it. It worked a treat and she picked it up as she rushed out, calling for Honesty to hurry as well.

As Mum rummaged in her purse for the key, she wore a puzzled expression on her face. Not worried, just puzzled. She said to Honesty, 'I'm getting so absent-minded! I could have sworn I had a bit more money in here. I hope I haven't dropped it somewhere.'

Honesty knew where the money had gone, of course. She had taken another fifty quid on Friday because she had seen this perfect bag for her school stuff – waterproof and with pictures of pop stars on it. She had been a bit taken aback at the price and needed to top up her cash to afford it.

They jumped in the car. Mum was still wondering out loud where the money had gone. Honesty just nodded and grunted and hoped that her face was not as red as her hair.

It was not long before Mum forgot the missing money (she was not one to go on about things she couldn't fix) and started on another subject (manufacturing standards).

Honesty, very aware that her coveted new bag had probably been made in precisely the sort of circumstances her mother was describing, snapped, 'It can't be that bad, Mum!'

She could tell that she had shocked Mum. She didn't usually contradict her and was hardly ever rude. But Mum didn't say anything. Honesty could almost see her decide to let it pass. Honesty sighed. She was certainly enjoying school a whole lot more but weekends were stressful.

At the market, they set up quickly and efficiently and were soon briskly selling – Honesty was too busy helping pack apples in brown paper bags and weighing asparagus on the old-fashioned scales to even look at the customers.

It was only when she heard a high, familiar voice exclaim, 'Honey! I was hoping to find you here. It's great to see you,' that Honesty looked up.

Her hands turned cold and her face drained of blood.

Caitlin, for that was who it was, turned to her mother and said, 'This is Honey, Mum. From school. She's my best friend.'

Then it happened, the question Honesty had feared from the moment she had heard Caitlin's voice, 'But why are you wearing those awful clothes again?'

And to her own mother, 'Honey has the whole new range of Pink Princess stuff, Mum. Remember I was asking for it and you said no? She even has the Powder Pink Power Puff jacket!'

Caitlin's Mum stuck a hand out to Honesty's Mum, 'These girls! I don't know how you cope with them always asking for everything in the shops. I have a terrible time with my Caitlin here. Anyway, it's a pleasure to meet you. Caitlin's been talking about Honey a lot recently.'

Honesty didn't wait to hear what Mum said. She didn't look up to see her expression. It felt like she had swallowed an entire organic apple. Her throat had a lump in it and her stomach hurt. She dropped the punnet of strawberries she was holding and took off.

It had been raining and the ground was muddy. It was early but there were already crowds of people at the market. Honesty ran fast, skidding and sliding and bumping into farmers and customers. She sped through a puddle at the entrance where the farmers parked their trucks for unloading and there were always tyre ruts collecting water. She splashed a woman who glared angrily after her and then started wiping down her poodle. Honesty could hear shouts and exclamations. She did not look back to see if it was Mum chasing her or if it was just angry shoppers yelling as she jostled and muddied them in her furious

94

exit. She raced through the car park packed with neat rows of mud-splattered cars. Once she reached a clear stretch of road, she glanced around hurriedly. There was no one in sight. But she would soon be spotted and picked up on the open road. Her sides hurt and the sweat on her brow felt chilly in the spring wind – like a cold compress against her forehead.

Every action of hers over the last two weeks was as clear as if she was re-living each moment, not just remembering it. She had stolen money from her own Mum. She had gorged on Big Macs and Whoppers. She had dressed in pink without a thought for the young girls in sweatshops hunched over sewing machines. She had hidden away her hand-sewn hemp dresses in bus station lockers. She had read nothing other than the TV Guide for a fortnight. And she had lied and lied and lied. How could Mum and Dad forgive her?

She could just imagine, in vivid detail, the conversation if she had stayed. Mum would've denied that her child owned anything pink from the shops and cheerfully explained her objections to mass-produced merchandise with references to Baiji dolphins and panda bears. Caitlin would describe her new wardrobe in detail. There would have been confusion. The whole group would have turned to look at Honesty for confirmation that there had been some sort of bizarre mix-up. Honesty could picture her Mum's face when she realised that Honesty was lying to her. Then Mum would remember the missing money. No, there was absolutely no going back.

That meant she had to decide where she was going next. The first thing to do was get off the road. Honesty hopped over a stile and made for the fields. In the distance she could see horses grazing. One of them might give her a lift.

• • •

Orang Tua led them through the forest. He was confident that he could lead them directly to the biggest camp. It was the base of a major plantation company. They were clearing land by burning acres of jungle. Soon they would start planting oil palms. The oil palm, which looks like a short squat coconut tree, was prized for its fruit (a watermelon-sized raspberry). The oil from the shiny red fruit was used for cooking. But humans were also keen to use it as a bio-fuel to replace fast dwindling oil supplies. Even the big oil companies were getting into the game, not wanting to be left behind if palm oil turned out to be the choice replacement for fossil fuels.

As they got closer, the animals could smell the fires. The air was thick with soot and dust. Visibility was poor. They could not find their way using the scent of the humans. The only smell in the air was the stench of burning vegetation. It made their eyes water and their throats hurt.

Gajah was suffering more than the others. His long trunk smarted with every breath he took. They had been warned to be silent by the rhino but Gajah sneezed. The sound came rocketing out of his trunk like the blast of a trumpet. The rhino signalled for them to stop and glared at Gajah who looked sheepish.

Harimau said in a low, rumbling, almost inaudible growl, 'We must go around. I know it is the sign of a poor hunter to be upwind of his prey but it is our best chance.'

The rhino nodded decisively. 'You're right. We will go around.'

He led the way and the air started to improve. They passed a pool of water, glinting green with the moss in its depths. Gajah sucked up a trunkful and then let it run out again. He let out a small sigh of relief. That was better. His trunk had really been hurting him. And he was terrified of jeopardising the mission with another sneezing fit.

The rhino sent Ular ahead. She slithered away hissing over her shoulder, 'Wisssh me luck. I don't want to end up as sssnake sssoup!'

Orang Tua gave her a thumbs up, a gesture he had seen a human use when he had strayed too close to a logging camp. He wondered whether the snake would be offended. It was difficult to know what behaviour was appropriate with such a motley crew of creatures. Still, it had been his idea to summon the Council of Beasts. They would all just have to be patient rather than take offence at every perceived insult. Ular did not seem bothered that Orang Tua had acted like a human. Her long tail was the last thing to disappear from view.

The animals sat around trying to ignore each other.

Geram ate a mango that he had picked on the way. The rhino grazed and occasionally muttered under his breath. Orang Tua hoped they had not made a mistake giving him command of the animal forces. His arrival at the Council was so talismanic, it had seemed the right thing to do. But the old ape was concerned that giving the job to the last member of his species might not have been the wisest decision. The rhino's interests did not coincide with their own. Most of them just wanted the space to live. The rhino wanted revenge.

The tiger was hungry. He glanced around at the herbivores in disgust, glowering at Geram in particular. The orang utan had mango juice running down his chin and was trying to wipe his sticky fingers on a large banana leaf.

Orang Tua followed the tiger's gaze as it lighted on Gajah who was gingerly flexing and unflexing his sore trunk. A soft hiss in his ear made him jump and he realised it was the King Cobra curled around a branch near his ear. The snake, unperturbed at the thought of the coming battle, was asleep and snoring gently, his forked tongue quivering with each breath. Orang Tua shivered. He knew that each of the creatures was only following its nature. Some beasts were carnivores. It was the way it was meant to be. Nobody could suggest that a beast as magnificent as the tiger should start eating vegetables. As for the cobra, it was a highly developed killing machine. It had the most toxic venom in the jungle and special jaws that could be unhinged to swallow its prey whole.

Orang Tua understood that there was nothing evil in following one's highly evolved nature. But that did not mean he was comfortable sitting within spitting distance of a pale, scaly cobra. He sidled down the branch to get further away. The snake woke up and stared at him. Orang Tua could have sworn that the creature had read his mind and knew his fears, its gaze was so knowing. He suppressed a shudder.

• • •

The eight-seater Cessna Caravan was a small, single-engine propeller aircraft. Spencer's Mum was gripping the armrests of the seat with both hands. Her knuckles were white and her nails red. Dad had his arms folded tightly across his chest. Spencer suspected he was trying to look tough to hide the fact that he was terrified. Spencer was not afraid. He loved bobbing amongst the clouds. It reminded him of being in a bouncy castle.

The drone of the small plane was immensely loud. It sounded like a Boeing 747 – except that they had arrived in Alaska on the big jumbo jet and it had been disappointingly quiet. The flight to Alaska was the first time Spencer had ever been on an aeroplane. Taking off was so cool. Poised at the end of the runway, rolling forward slowly. Accelerating. Long before Spencer had thought they were going fast enough, the plane had raised its nose into the air and gracefully and quietly taken to the skies. If he had not had his nose pressed firmly against the heavy duty double windows, Spencer would not have known they were airborne. There was some cool turbulence as they broke through the first layer of cloud. But after that, it was so quiet and monotonous that he had slept and missed the orange juice in a plastic container, the sandwich wrapped in cling film and the pilot's announcement that they were cruising at twenty eight thousand feet – all the things that he had been really looking forward to.

But this plane ride from Anchorage to the little encampment that was going to be their home for the next six months was more like the real thing. The aircraft dropped twenty feet and Spencer's stomach bounced into his throat and then back again – or at least that's what it felt like. Dad gave a little yelp and forgot to look firm and brave. Mum turned a pale shade of green that clashed with her smart red suit. Spencer laughed out loud. Mum glared at him.

The pilot, a huge, burly man squashed into his seat and pressed up against the controls, glanced back into the cabin and smiled at Spencer. Spencer grinned back, full of fellow feeling for this man who owned the skies. It did not stop him wondering how the pilot had ever managed to take off – there did not seem to be any room for him to pull back the stick without stabbing himself in the gut.

Far too quickly, they were skimming across the top of a wide, blue lake like a dragonfly over a pond. The water was completely still and as reflective as a mirror. Spencer could see the reflection of their plane rushing to keep up with them. It made him feel a tiny bit dizzy if he stared at it too hard. He stared at it some more to see if he would turn the same shade of green as his mother but was distracted by the pilot shouting over the noise of the throbbing engine. 'Belt up!' he yelled. 'We're going in.'

To his delight, Spencer realised they were going to land on the water. He saw, examining the speeding image in the water, two parallel water skis. He wasn't sure where to look in his excitement – the horizon, the lake, the plane's reflection, the pilot easing the controls downward. He spared a glance at his parents and discovered they both had their eyes shut. 'Mum! Dad! You have to see this. We're landing on the water!'

Mum muttered, 'That's why my eyes are shut.'

Dad maintained a thoughtful silence.

The little plane bounced and skipped over the surface of the water as spray flew past the windows. It slowed down slightly and then a bit more. The Cessna came to a gentle stop. The propeller was turning so furiously that individual blades were indistinguishable. But now the outline of each was visible as the revolutions became slower. The three blades stopped completely, the plane rocked gently on the waters and silence reigned.

It took the 'phut phut' of the outboard engine on a little boat to rouse everyone.

'That's your lift,' said the pilot cheerfully.

'Aren't you coming?' asked Spencer.

'No way, young man. Can't leave my ship out here.' (It took Spencer a moment to realise he was talking about his plane.)

'Looks mighty quiet right now but this lake can heave like an ocean when the wind's up. Ain't no place to park a plane.'

'But what if we need to leave?' asked his Mum plaintively.

'There's a radio at the camp and I come in every week with supplies. You don't have to worry your pretty little head. Just holler and I'll be right back.'

The family clambered out of the aircraft and balanced on the skis. The boat was getting closer. Spencer could see it was piloted by a man with a heavy beard wearing dark sunglasses as protection against the glare of the sun on the waters. He waved a greeting as he pulled up alongside the plane. Spencer's mother was assisted into the boat where she sat down with a sigh of relief and shaded her eyes to watch the progress of her husband and son. Dad stepped into the boat, rocked back and forth trying to get his balance and then sat down suddenly and painfully. Spencer leapt nimbly into the boat, balanced on his heels like an old pro, made his way to the prow and knelt down. He peered over the side into the water to see if he could spot any big fish.

Mum asked nervously, 'Anything dangerous in there?' as Spencer trailed his fingers in the water.

'No, ma'am. Nothing except our dinner once in a while.'

The two men efficiently stacked the bags in the boat, the boatman pulled on the cord, the outboard engine burst into life and they chugged towards the shore. The pilot gave them a last cheery wave, squeezed himself back into the plane and was soon accelerating across the waters, leaving two parallel white-topped trails in his wake. The ripples from his progress rocked the boat. Spencer's Mum grabbed his Dad and looked into the water in alarm. Spencer had his eyes glued to the Cessna as it took off. The plane did a tight circle, flew overhead, the pilot waved once and then was gone.

'Awesome!' said Spencer and he meant it.

• • •

Elliot Valentine sat in an empty boardroom. Tarzan was asleep at his feet. The table in front of him was round and had been specially made for him from the massive felled trunk of the largest single tree ever discovered in the United States, one of the giant sequoia that grew in Yellowstone Park. He traced the outline of a whorl, polished smooth but still visible in the grain, with his finger.

The boardroom was filling up. His assistants were filing in, politely saying 'Good afternoon, Mr. Valentine' as they came in. Last to arrive were Mr. Smooth, whose name was actually Deakin, and Mr. Rough, whose name was Bent. They took the seats on the right and left side of their boss. There was complete silence except for the nervous shuffling of bums on seats.

Valentine glanced around the room. He was pleased with the team he had put together. They were smart, ambitious, greedy and terrified of him. And now the final jigsaw piece was in place.

He said, 'I've found him and sent him to Alaska.'

'That scientist guy?' asked Mr. Deakin.

Valentine inclined his head and a few more chins appeared under his jaw.

'You think he's up to the job?' Mr. Bent was the only man in the room who was prepared to question Valentine's judgment.

Valentine was confident. 'He's the man that's going to find me lots of black gold under the Alaskan ice and snow.'

'The newspapers are up in arms about your plans to explore Alaska's wildlife reserves looking for oil,' remarked Mr. Deakin.

'A few politicians are jumping on the bandwagon as well,' added an aide.

Elliot Valentine had no doubt that his powerful oil lobby would find a way through any resistance. He firmly believed that there was nothing in the world that could not be bought or stolen.

He said confidently, 'I'll handle that.'

There were a few doubtful faces around the table.

Valentine continued, 'I am going to build oil platforms and refineries and pipelines wherever there is a single drop of oil to be sucked out of the ground. As to these do-gooders whining about the caribou and the polar bears, they'll change their tune when they realise they might have to bike down Pennsylvania Avenue if they stand in my way.'

'And when the fossil fuels run out? When you've extracted every drop out of every wilderness across the whole planet? What happens next?' asked Mr. Bent.

'You know – that's a very good question.' Valentine grinned and his cheeks bunched up into two rotten, wrinkled apples.

All eyes were on the fat man.

'What comes after oil? Bio-fuels, I think. And I've just bought a billion-dollar company with oil palm plantations right across Borneo. And I'm closing a deal for corn plantations in the Amazon. I'm going to plant oil palms and corn across every last bit of rainforest and when the oil runs out … I'm going to sell folks all the bio-fuels they need.'

The room burst into spontaneous applause. There was a reason that Elliot Valentine was considered the most talented businessman of his generation. They felt privileged to watch him in action.

Valentine waited for the clapping to stop and then said, 'Deakin, I want you in the Amazon. Bent – you go to Borneo. There's work to be done.'

Bent almost smiled.

Valentine patted his wolf on the head. 'Everything is going to plan, Tarzan,' he said. The wolf yawned.

-fifteen-

Honesty persuaded a mare in the field to give her a lift. The horse was reluctant to leave her paddock but Honesty convinced her that it was urgent. At last, the mare agreed, warning her two young foals to behave while she was away and not to try and squeeze through any gaps in the hedge.

They clumped along over the fields in silence until the mare asked, 'Where are we going, exactly?'

Honesty was surprised to find a horse capable of asking a lucid question but she answered honestly enough, 'I'm not sure yet. I just needed to get away.'

'But you're just a foal, aren't you?'

Honesty nodded and then realised that the horse could not see her head as she sat high on its back. She said, 'Yes, I am.'

'I don't think you should be on your own then.'

Honesty said sadly, 'I have no choice. I did something pretty dreadful. I can't go back.'

'Well, maybe humans are different. But there is nothing my foals could do that I would not forgive, and Betsy made

106

a real mess of her coat last week squeezing through the hedge and she got lost and caused me and Farmer Brown no end of worry.'

Honesty thought about everything she had done in the last two weeks and two big tears rolled down her cheeks and plopped on the mare's back.

The mare looked up anxiously, 'I hope it's not going to rain.'

In the end, Honesty decided on London. She needed to hide and to earn some money. London was the place to be. She thought of all the books she had read – of chimney sweeps and heroes, of prime ministers and abolitionists and of wartime and magic. Perhaps she might be able to make up for what she had done. Find a way to earn Mum's forgiveness. London was definitely the place to go if you were eleven years old and had messed up really badly.

The mare dropped her on the outskirts of the nearest town with a railway line. Honesty flung her arms around the mare's neck and hugged her tightly. The horse whinnied and nuzzled her and wished her luck. Honesty resolutely turned her back on the animal and followed the track down towards the small station she could see in the distance. She was in luck. The path by the track led directly onto the platform. There were people milling about but they were all looking down the line to where the rumble of a train could be heard in the distance. The electronic sign hanging from the roof read, 'LONDON, 3 MINS'.

Honesty had never felt so lonely in her life. She saw

a large, happy family wrestling with its luggage and its babies. She followed them on board and sat as close as she dared. The train drew slowly out of the station.

The mare watched Honesty walk down the track until she disappeared from view. Then she neighed a quiet goodbye and turned to canter back to her foals. She was worried about the girl. No good ever came of young ones leaving their mothers before they were ready. She had foaled three times and knew that well. The mare flared her nostrils and blew out a regretful sigh.

A hunched, mottled buzzard sitting on the branch of a wild cherry tree asked inquisitively, 'What's up?'

The mare was deep in thought and said absently, 'Worried about that child.'

'Why?'

'She's one of those. You know, she can talk to animals. But she's run away from home.'

'Talk to animals?'

'Yes, you must have heard of such humans. Animal Talkers. They understand us. Us creatures, I mean.'

The buzzard said thoughtfully, 'Yes, I have heard of them. She's one, is she?'

The mare whinnied.

'How interesting,' said the buzzard and flew off in such a hurry that a few of its tail feathers fell off and drifted slowly to the ground.

• • •

Ular's summary was brief and to the point. As was often the case when he was apprehensive or in a hurry, his sibilant accent was pronounced.

'The camp isss large. Over fifty men. They're all working to clear the foressst. Some of them are lighting the firesss. Others are controlling the direction of the burn with firebreaks and water. Patches that have been burnt to the ground are being cleared by metal monsters with huge teeth. The scorched ground is sssmoking and too hot for any of us. I stayed in the trees.'

'What about living quarters?' asked Gajah.

'They have tents and caravans. In rowsss. Pitched along the river.'

'How far is the camp from the leading edge of the fire?' asked the rhino.

'Twenty minutes hard ssslithering,' said Ular, raising his body so they could see the bruises and missing scales on his underside.

'They're not stupid,' said Orang Tua. 'They burn down-wind of the camp.'

Gajah said snidely, 'If they were stupid, we wouldn't be on the verge of extinction.'

'Firesticks?' asked Harimau in an extra gruff voice to hide his fear.

'They all have them.'

A silence met this last comment.

'There's more, I'm afraid,' said Ular quietly.

The others looked at him curiously.

'There are elephants.'

'What do you mean?' trumpeted Gajah angrily.

'There are elephants working with the humans. Helping to clear the land. Not pygmy elephants though, full-sized ones.'

The animals hung their heads.

Gajah look distressed and swung his trunk from side to side. His voice shook. 'They catch our young and train them and put them to work …'

Orang Tua patted him on the side comfortingly.

'We know that the elephants would not choose to be there, Gajah. Our own people have terrible tales of baby orang utans stolen and brought up as human children. They are even made to wear clothes!'

Geram drew back his lips, bared his fruit-stained teeth and shrieked in anger.

Only the rhino stayed focussed.

'Do you think they will help us?'

'Who?' asked Ular, confused.

'The elephants. Will they help us?'

Ular wriggled uncertainly. 'I don't know.'

Gajah shook his head. 'You know what happens to animals in captivity. They are lost to us, I think.'

'Perhaps some of the younger ones might retain a memory of their wild past?' asked Orang Tua.

'Perhaps,' said Gajah. 'I am not hopeful.'

The rhino said, 'Well, they will have to choose now. They are either with us or against us. There is no in between.'

The others fell silent. None of them had considered the possibility of having to fight animals as well as humans.

It was Harimau who gave voice to their thoughts, 'If we war with other *beasts* – are we any better than the humans?'

• • •

Spencer had not thought he would ever be happy again after killing Achak. But he was. Alaska suited him. Wide open spaces. Air so crisp it felt like a solid thing, a wall perhaps, or when it was hurting his nostrils, a pair of sharp tweezers pulling at his nose hair. The lake was an adventure in itself. He soon learnt to use the small dinghy with the outboard motor. Mum was really nervous about him going out on his own. But she let him. She was too pleased to see him cheerful to stand in his way.

Spencer loved to go out in the dinghy and land on a shore, some distance from the camp. He would take a sandwich, tie the shoelaces on his hiking boots extra tight and go for long walks. He had a compass and he knew that he could always climb a tree to locate the lake if he got lost. But he never did. He knew from the smell of the wind and the colour of the leaves, the direction he should go. He could even tell the time from the position of the sun. Spencer was very proud of this particular skill. He would squint at the sun, one hand sheltering his eyes from the intensity of the glare and say importantly, 'It's just after twelve, Mum.' She would be genuinely amazed. His parents loved the fresh air and quiet after the hustle and bustle of New York City. But they were town folk on a trip to the country. Spencer was a country boy.

Occasionally, he would spot an animal. Out of the corner of his eye, there would be a flash of brown fur. A grizzly, perhaps. Or maybe a moose. He wished he could get close. But the creatures were nervous of people. And, if he was honest, he was hesitant to approach them. He was terrified of speaking to one of the creatures and getting no answer that he understood. Spencer was beginning to doubt whether the conversation with the deer in the forest had actually taken place. Maybe he had dreamt the whole thing. Not shooting the poor beast. He knew that was real. When he remembered Achak the pain in his chest was so intense it almost felt like he'd been shot too. But speaking to the deer first? He must have drifted off to sleep and dreamt it. Funny that he had been so sure.

Spencer could see Dad was happy too. He was working hard on the soil samples, geological surveys and maps, trying to find the oil lurking under the surface – and the best way of getting it out. The next step after this would be to head to the tundra and look at the ground itself – to see whether his predictions were accurate.

Once in a while, Valentine would call to check on progress. Mention of Valentine always turned Spencer silent. He couldn't help himself. His stomach would tie itself into knots and he would develop a lump in his throat that made it really hard to speak. Mum would glare at Dad as if to say, why are you bringing up that ghastly man when you know how our boy reacts. The subject of Elliot Valentine became taboo in the house. They received his wages, did his work and lived at his research facility, but they never spoke of him.

• • •

Honesty disembarked at Victoria Station and, using the same large family for cover, snuck past the attendant checking tickets at the platform exit. She had never been to London before. She was petrified by the vastness of the station. It had arched roofs and crowds of hurried, worried people rushing about their business. None of them noticed Honesty. They walked past her, staring ahead, looking for signboards and platforms. It was as if she was invisible. She felt horribly alone and out of place. A fat grey pigeon flew by, clumsy but fast, and much too close.

People were looking at a large display where the train times and destinations were flashing up and changing with bewildering regularity. Honesty went to gaze at it too. It gave her something to do while deciding her next step. It was already late evening and she needed somewhere to stay. But she had to look after her money until she found a way of adding to it. Honesty had read enough to know that her best bet was pick-pocketing or begging – she did not think hiring herself out as a chimney sweep was possible anymore. She looked at the board again. The trains did not run all night which meant the station would eventually be deserted. It would be too scary to hang around when the place was empty.

Honesty saw a booth advertising London hotels and went over. The highly-painted woman behind the counter looked at her with complete disinterest and said, 'Yes, can I help you?' in a voice that indicated it was the last thing she wanted to do.

Honesty put on her most adult voice and said, 'I was just wondering how much the cheapest room for the night would cost?'

'Just one night?'

'Yes, please.'

'Thirty pounds including VAT.'

Honesty tried to keep the shock off her face. Thirty pounds! She only had a fifty. And what was VAT? A large container – but of what?

'If I don't want a VAT, would it be cheaper?'

'None of us want VAT, ducky.' The woman straightened up and looked at her suspiciously. 'Where are your parents anyway?'

Honesty looked around hastily. She gestured in the direction of a distant family with a bawling baby and said, 'Over there. Mum just sent me over to check the prices because the baby's acting up.'

The woman nodded and looked slightly more sympathetic. 'You wouldn't think it to look at me but I have a couple of brats myself. They're at home with my Mum. Their Dad's long gone, of course. The same with you lot, I suppose?'

Honesty nodded sadly, hoping no loving father would turn up to attend to the unknown family. She felt a pang of longing for her own big, warm, comfy Dad.

'Well, if you're really short of a bob or two, your best bet is to look for a youth hostel. They're plain, but cheap and clean.'

Honesty said, 'We're pretty desperate, I'm afraid. We only have fifty quid.'

The woman shook her head at that.

'That is desperate. I guess your Mum has come out looking for your old man? She should take it from me – she's better off without him.'

Honesty stayed silent.

'OK – here's what you do …'

Honesty was all ears.

'Go to the airport.'

'The airport? I don't want to go anywhere else!'

'No, no. One of the airports, like Gatwick – not Heathrow and their bloody security alerts. It's the best place to doss down. People assume you have an early flight.'

It made sense. It would be quite safe and she would not look out of place, not if she found another large family to hang around.

She smiled at her new best friend in London, 'Thanks very much. I'll tell Mum.'

The woman at the booth fished under the counter and re-appeared with a squashy bar of chocolate. She handed it to Honesty.

Honesty took it. She was starving.

A queue had formed behind her and she stepped aside. The man behind her moved forward and leaned on the counter.

'Do I get some chocolate too?' he asked.

The hotel lady giggled and simpered.

• • •

Orang Tua asked, 'Do we go in tonight?'

There was a quick shake of the head from the rhino. 'We will wait here for three days to make sure we understand their routine.'

'Three days! But I'm famished,' growled Harimau hungrily, eyeing Gajah who took a few hasty steps back.

'I know,' said the rhino. 'I want us all to be hungry. A hungry animal is alert and tense. A well-fed beast is sleepy and inert. We need to be at our most aggressive. Our instincts at their most acute. Our bellies must be empty for our own good.'

'You may be right,' Gajah said plaintively, 'but you have to get that tiger to stop looking at me. It's making me nervous.'

They all laughed, even Harimau. He said in a growly, smiley voice, 'You're much too tough for me.'

-sixteen-

The buzzard told a barn owl. The barn owl stared fixedly at the buzzard, yellow eyes glowing in the evening light.

'Why are you telling me?' she asked.

'Because there's no time to waste. It's late in the day already. And you can fly at night.'

'What's in it for me?'

The buzzard did not answer. The barn owl was not endangered. It was not her fight.

'If the beasts need an Animal Talker, why don't you just talk to the girl yourself?'

'The Borneo apes are in charge,' explained the buzzard. 'I'm not sure why they want an Animal Talker. Something about finding some Seeds that might help creatures that are almost extinct. We've been told to send word ... not take matters into our own wings. Besides, the girl has run away. I have no idea where she is now.'

The barn owl made a fluting, hooting sound. It took a moment for the buzzard to realise she was laughing.

'I'll carry the message,' she said. 'Barn owls may be

alright. But my mother's side of the family includes some Asiatic eagle owls. And there aren't many of them left, that's for sure.'

With a swift powerful upward thrust of her big, feathery wings, the owl took to the sky. The buzzard watched her silhouette grow smaller against the setting sun. Then he put his head under his wing and went to sleep. It had been a long day.

The owl flew silently towards the sea. Her great wings beat with quiet rhythm. Her great eyes pierced the darkness to spot mice scurrying for cover and bats duck and weave between the trees. She was tempted to stop for a snack but did not. This was not the time for picnics.

She reached the shore as the sun rose. The ebony horizon was infused with a maidenly pink blush. The sea that had been a sheet of black glass meeting the black wall of the night was starting to show texture – ripples as it rushed to shore and ruffles where the wind caught the surface. The sun broke cover over the horizon and the world was renewed. The white cliffs of Dover sparkled and shone. But the owl was not interested in nature's splendour. She was tired. She was hungry. And she was keen to pass on the responsibility for her message.

She scanned the horizon anxiously. Not an eagle in sight. The skies were as clear as in the days before birds had evolved from ground creatures. But the buzzard's instructions were quite clear. The barn owl had to find a sea-eagle and tell it that they had found an Animal

Talker. The owl hooted in frustration. So many species of animals were on the brink of extinction and this kid who could talk to the animals had run away from home and was wandering around London. London! Not a place for a child or an animal. If they were to enlist her in the cause, they would need to rescue her first.

The owl took another turn out to sea. There were still no eagles. Where in the world were these lazy birds? The owl's eyes hurt as the sun grew brighter over the horizon. Her pupils narrowed against the glare but her vision was starting to blur. Owls were nocturnal creatures. They were not supposed to be flying around as the day began, looking for some good-for-nothing eagles.

She addressed a loud, urgent hoot to an empty sky. 'Can anyone hear me?'

A voice replied from directly under her, 'Yes, I can actually. There's no need to shout.'

The owl squinted and peered down towards the water. There was nothing to be seen. She flew a bit closer and was immediately sprayed with a fine mist of water as a humpback whale spouted out of his blowhole. Tired and bedraggled from her long flight, her eyes sore from the light and now with sodden feathers, the owl was struggling. She felt disoriented and heavy, her powerful wings not strong enough to keep her airborne. She flapped valiantly.

The whale, watching the owl's increasingly futile efforts said, 'Steady there, steady. Are you alright?'

The owl did not answer. Her claws brushed the water.

This provoked another brave attempt to escape. She managed, with a supreme effort, to rise a few feet above the surface but a wave caught her wingtip and it was over. She was in the salty water. There was some residual buoyancy left in her wings and she bobbed on the surface. And then sank.

The whale moved quickly. He slipped under the water. Then he rose up, careful not to break surface too violently. He slid out of the sea as smoothly as the owl herself had slid through the night. He came up under the bird. One moment the owl was sliding into the blackness of the undersea, the next moment she was perched on the back of a humpback whale. Neither creature said anything. The whale was trying to float on the waters with minimum movement, using his huge tail to maintain a still platform for the unfortunate owl.

The owl was astounded. Had she just been rescued by a whale? If so, to what end? Did whales eat owls? She didn't think so. But neither, as far as she was aware, did they rescue drowning owls. The owl postponed worrying about the whale's motives and concentrated on getting dry. She fluffed up her feathers and shook herself thoroughly. It was not quite water off a duck's back (she was an owl, after all), but it was a good start. She felt light again, like a creature of the air. She had to shut her eyes though. The sun had risen and it was very bright on the open seas.

The whale said, politely, but pointedly, 'I hope you're not falling asleep up there.'

The owl denied this hastily, 'No, of course not. It's just a bit bright, that's all.'

'So you are nocturnal,' said the whale, pleased to have spotted this. 'But what were you doing out to sea hooting and yelling at daybreak?'

The owl sighed. 'You wouldn't believe me if I told you.'

'Try me! I'm on a fairly ridiculous mission myself.'

'Really?' asked the owl, opening her eyes a slit in surprise. 'What are you up to?'

The whale rocked to and fro in embarrassment and the owl had to dig her talons into his back to keep hold.

'Hey, watch it. Owww!' exclaimed the whale.

'Sorry. I was afraid of falling!'

The whale whistled a gracious acceptance of this apology.

The owl asked again, 'So what are you doing?'

'I'm looking for an Animal Talker,' said the whale.

The owl was silent and the whale continued, looking shamefaced, 'I told you it was silly.'

'No, it isn't,' hooted the owl earnestly.

'Why not?'

'Because I've found one.'

• • •

Honesty took the train to Gatwick Airport, buying a cheap return ticket out of her small stash of cash. The terminal building was brightly lit and there were enough people about that Honesty did not feel afraid. Hungry, tired, lonely and very sad, yes. But not afraid. She spent an uncomfortable night trying to sleep on a row of hard plastic seats. Every time she drifted off to sleep someone would sit down or get up and the whole row of seats would shake.

The airport awoke for the morning rush very early. Honesty was grateful that she did not have to keep trying for a sleep that would not come. Instead, she got up, dusted herself off, stretched like a cat after a nap and went to the bathroom to wash up. She felt awful. Her neck was stiff. Her fingers were numb with cold. Her mouth tasted like she'd been chewing on Dad's socks. She had no toothbrush. She washed her face and ran watery hands through her hair until the cold trickles on her scalp woke her fully. She flattened her hair as much as possible and dusted off the hemp clothes, trying to make them look less crumpled.

An angry growl caught her attention. It was her stomach. She needed food. She was famished. Her money wouldn't last very long if she was hungry the whole time. Honesty decided to have a hearty breakfast (Mum always said that a good meal first thing in the morning could get you through the day) and not bother with food after that. The thought of her Mum made her feel a bit tearful but she wiped her eyes furiously with her knuckles, squared her skinny shoulders, glared at herself in the mirror (she had red eyes to match the hair) and marched out in pursuit of breakfast.

A dreadful (in health terms) but delicious (for a hungry

eleven year old) meal of fried chicken and chips made her feel strong enough to take on the world. Honesty made up her mind. She would head back to London and try and find a way of earning some money. She hunted around and found the return ticket crumpled in a pocket.

Honesty stepped out of the station onto a crowded London street. Everyone seemed busy and angry. People were striding about shouting into mobile phones. Eleven year old runaways were quite likely to get trodden on, thought Honesty, as she tried to get out of the way of a big, red-faced man waving his briefcase in front of him like a weapon. Honesty hid in the doorway of a grey and stately building. She put out a hand and touched the stone wall. It was as cold and forbidding as it looked. A doorman in a tall hat and a coat with tails waggled a finger at her, 'You, girl. I don't know what you're doing but go do it somewhere else.'

Honesty hurried across the road and was chuffed to see that there were notices on many shop windows advertising for waitresses and kitchen help. She walked into Joe's Fish and Chips. The place reeked of fish oil and vinegar.

Honesty said timidly to a small man with long muscular arms and a dirty apron, 'Please, I'd like to be a waitress?'

'Hey Joe! This kid wants to be a waitress!'

Joe turned around from frying chips, looked Honesty up and down and snorted with amusement.

Honesty said desperately, 'I can work really hard.'

The man with the long arms said in an almost kindly

tone, 'Hiring kids is against the law, like. You'd best get back to school now.'

There was a man fast asleep, curled up on flattened cardboard boxes at the entrance to a London Underground station. He was unkempt with a long, matted, curling beard. His clothes were tattered and grimy. People dropped a coin or two by his head but he did not stir. He had a mangy, piebald mongrel dog guarding his sleeping form. Honesty had a horrid, sinking feeling that she would soon be in the same position. Except without a dog to look out for her.

'What are you looking at?' snapped the dog.

Honesty looked around to see if the dog could be speaking to anyone else and said, 'Nothing! Honestly, nothing.'

'Then bugger off.'

• • •

Humans would kill a cobra on sight, regardless of whether they knew that the cobra was on the attack. One of the most venomous snakes in Borneo, a cobra was only dangerous within the range of its lunge. To kill, a cobra had to sink its fangs deep into the skin of its prey and release the poison from the special glands behind its teeth into the flesh. A man with a gun standing twenty feet away from a cobra was as safe as houses.

The biggest male cobra slithered through the undergrowth picking his way through the rotting leaves and fallen branches. He could feel the stillness of the ground. If anything stirred, he would sense the vibrations through his skin.

Geram had not been pleased with the rhino's plan for the cobras. They were to slither into the camp, find the tents and caravans of the foremen (not difficult – the bosses always had the best of everything that they could drag into the jungle) and bite them while they slept. If they did not have anti-venom stocks at the camp, the leaders would die within fifteen minutes. If they did have the anti-venom, they might live – but they would not be in a position to lead any fight.

The plan offended Geram's sense of fair play. He was here to fight, not murder people in their beds. But the others had scoffed at his scruples. As the rhino pointed out dryly, 'As long as the humans have firesticks, you don't have to worry about a fair fight.'

• • •

Spencer could hardly breathe, he was so excited. His heart thumped, his eyes sparkled and he kept wiping his hands against his shorts.

He asked, 'Can you see the plane?'

His Mum put her arm around her son's slender shoulders and gave him a quick tight hug.

'I'm sure it'll be here soon.'

She looked at her husband over the boy's head. He was

smiling too. Richard looked around. It was truly amazing. It felt like being alive for the first time. The mountains with their snowy caps and forests of spruce and birch, the lake looking like one giant sapphire, glinting and gleaming in the sun as the light caught the waters.

The view was briefly clouded by a clear, stark memory of the skinned deer with a bullet hole in its side. Richard was suddenly afraid of the Alaskan beauty all around. This was not a holiday picture postcard. It was Nature. And where Man and Nature met, there was always conflict. Richard tried to shake off the feeling of impending catastrophe that had darkened his mood so abruptly.

The plane landed and father and son clambered aboard with two other members of the research team. His Mum waved furiously as they took off into the sunny blue wilderness of the sky. They were going to collect ice and soil samples from north of the Arctic Circle. Using the equipment carefully wrapped in waterproof oilskins, Spencer's Dad was intent on prospecting for oil. Spencer didn't care about any of that. He had only one thought in his mind. He might see a polar bear. A great, big, massive, fearsome polar bear. He bounced up and down in his seat, he was too buzzed up to sit still.

• • •

Gajah left the others and went to talk to the captive elephants. He did not hold out much hope of persuading them to abandon their human masters. But he had insisted that he had to make the effort.

Even a pygmy elephant is too big to be entirely silent in the jungle. Gajah made his way as quietly as he could, keeping an eye out for the cobras. His big feet crackled through the dry leaves and once he snapped a twig. The sound was like a gunshot. Gajah almost fainted from the shock. He took a few minutes to examine his body for bullet wounds. He had not been shot, not yet anyway. Gajah set off again. He knew from Ular's report where the elephants were gathered – each with a thick rope looped around one massive leg, the other end tied to a tree.

It was not long before he could smell the elephants. He had to suppress the desire to trumpet a greeting. He doubted there would be a human on guard – captive elephants became docile very quickly. But the rhino had emphasised the importance of being careful and Gajah planned to follow his instructions to the letter.

He got as close as he could to the elephants and then whispered a formal greeting, 'By the length of my trunk, I am pleased to find my brothers here.'

Some of the elephants were asleep, lying on the ground with their eyes shut. But a few were awake, staring into the blackness or chewing on long pieces of grass.

These looked at him, bewildered. One of them seemed to remember the old greeting and responded, 'By the flap of my ears, you are welcome here.'

Another interrupted, 'Well, he's not really, is he?'

'What do you mean?' asked a third.

'What would we want with him? He's a pygmy, too small for hard work ... and we have plenty of hard work in the morning.'

'Are you here to join us?' asked the she-elephant who had remembered the words of welcome. 'You do look a bit puny.'

Gajah, small of size but large of temper, was getting annoyed.

'Join you?' he snapped. 'I'm here to rescue you!'

This provoked an outbreak of mirth that woke the sleeping elephants. They all gathered around as far as their tethers would allow them.

'Rescue us?' an elephant asked. 'From what?'

'A lifetime of slavery, perhaps?'

'It's just a job,' grumbled one of them.

'And what do you get out of it?' asked Gajah angrily. 'Some dry grass and your own six feet of rope?'

There were angry rumbles at this. Gajah knew he was approaching the elephants, with their overdeveloped sense of dignity and pride, completely wrong. But he was furious at being called puny.

'Besides,' he continued. 'It's not just a job when you're destroying our homes, is it?'

'It's just a few trees in a big rainforest,' snapped the biggest elephant. 'We're not doing much damage.'

Gajah was so inflamed he could barely speak. He stomped his feet, flapped his ears and swung his trunk from side to side in disgust. 'Not doing much damage? Have you guys been working in the sun too much? Or been drinking fermented coconut water?'

'Watch it, you little pipsqueak. How dare you come in here and start calling us names? What do you want anyway?' This question was put to Gajah by an aggressive looking male who was starting to strain angrily at his rope. Gajah moved out of range before replying, 'I told you. I'm here to rescue you.'

'We don't need to be rescued, thanks.'

'Look,' said Gajah determinedly. 'The animals are fighting back. We are attacking tonight. You are my people. I don't want you to be caught in between.'

'Your people?' snorted a big, grey, wrinkled beast. 'We're elephants with a job to do. You're some sort of small circus freak. Now get away from here before you get hurt by the grown-ups!'

Gajah was so incensed, he charged at the big beast. With one swoop the big grey knocked him to one side with his trunk and his tusks. Fortunately for Gajah he was knocked out of range or they would have trampled him to death there and then.

He got to his feet shakily. It was a powerful body blow and he was bleeding from where the elephant's tusks had gouged his side. Gajah looked at the elephants sorrowfully. 'I'm sorry you feel like that. I will fight to free you and all our kind from the certain destruction that faces us.'

There was no response from the herd. One by one they

went back to whatever they had been doing. Some lay down and shut their eyes to sleep. The big, aggressive elephant lowered his head and shook his trunk threateningly at Gajah and then turned his back on the pygmy. Gajah watched them for a while from the sidelines hoping one of them, just one, might see things his way. It was a vain hope. He walked back into the rainforest with a bleeding side and an aching heart.

-seventeen-

Valentine felt confident. All the signs were good. The Chinese government had signed a deal with Texic for a fifty-year supply of biofuels from oil palm plantations in Borneo. They were keen to phase out the coal-fired plants that were fouling the air around major cities like Beijing and Shanghai. It would take thousands of acres of new plantations to match that demand. It was fantastic. Valentine could not have hoped for such success so quickly.

On top of that, he had just seen the maps produced by Richard Jones of the most likely sources of new oil in Alaska. There was an apologetic note at the bottom pointing out that the best areas were in wildlife conservation districts on the North Shore and therefore off-limits to drilling.

Valentine did his giggly, chuckling, fat-trembling thing. Wildlife conservation districts? He ran his stubby fingers through the short rough hair on Tarzan's neck. The wolf yelped and snapped as a diamond ring got caught in his skin. Valentine laughed even louder, patted the animal again and gave him a chocolate biscuit. Then he had one himself. It did not take long for the two of them to finish the packet. Valentine sat back in his big leather chair while the wolf snuffled around the packet trying to lick the chocolate stuck to the sides with his long, pink tongue.

• • •

Geram and Orang Tua went in together. Their mission was straightforward. They had to destroy those strange growling, vibrating machines that sent light to the small moons strung out above the camp. But neither of them knew what to do. How did one fight one of these machines? It was not alive, so how could it die?

'Perhaps,' said Geram, 'They can be broken.'

Orang Tua shook his head, 'I don't think so. I have seen pieces of these machines left in the forest by men when their work is done. They are harder than the wood of the teak tree. They will not break.'

'Then what are we going to do?'

'We will have to find a way.'

The orang utans fell silent. They knew they were getting closer because the glow from the camp was visible through the trees. It darkened the shadows. The orang utans crept forward, clinging to the night as they had once clung to their mothers. They reached the camp and quietly, at ground level, they parted the leaves to have a look. It was deep into the night so all was still at the camp and silent –

except for the racket made by the machines they had come to destroy. Orang Tua counted them quickly.

'I can see two,' he whispered.

Geram nodded.

'Shall we split up?' Geram asked.

Orang Tua thought for a moment, scratching a tuft of hair on his chest with his long thin fingers.

'No,' he said. 'Not yet. Let's work out how to stop one of these machines together.'

The two orang utans crawled through the undergrowth along the perimeter of the camp. They moved silently using their knuckles for balance. Geram put a hand on Orang Tua's back and gestured at the trees. Orang Tua shook his head. They would be more comfortable off the ground. But they were not far from the first generator and there was no point taking the long route.

They could feel the vibrations on the ground and smell the diesel fumes in the air. The machine was old and greasy.

Geram moved forward bravely until he was within reach. He put out one long, hairy finger and touched the machine. Immediately he skittered back, screaming angrily.

'Shhhh!' said Orang Tua.

Geram held up the finger to show Orang Tua the blister that was already forming from contact with the hot surface. His face contorted in pain and he put his finger in his mouth.

It was Orang Tua's turn to have a look. He slunk forward, careful not to touch anything. His nerves were stretched taut. He was terrified. Terrified of the humans and their firesticks. Terrified of their plan to fight back. And most of all, most immediately, terrified of this ugly rumbling, groaning man-machine that stank so unnaturally.

• • •

The owl was on her way home. She had stayed with the whale, whose name was Kai, until a sea-eagle had finally put in an appearance. The barn owl had whooped and hollered and the whale had sung his heart out until they had caught the attention of the bird.

The eagle had swooped down in surprise at the summons. She too had perched on the whale, trying not to sink her powerful talons into the whale's blubbery back. Kai took his new role as bird carrier philosophically. These small indignities were worth the price, if he could be part of the effort to fight back against Man.

The sea-eagle had listened with growing excitement to their story. They had made a plan quickly, all of them being decisive creatures by nature and necessity. No beast survived in the wild except by knowing how to make life and death decisions immediately. Animals constantly balanced the never-ending hunt for food against the risks. Was it safe to swoop for that fish or was it too close to the trawlers? Was that a shadow in the water or a massive net strung out across the bottom of the ocean? Was that mouse a good choice for dinner or was it being chased by a cat that would seize the chance to practice its hunting skills on an owl? Creatures that got the answers wrong were dead.

The sea-eagle agreed immediately to carry the word of the Animal Talker as far as she could go and then pass it on to other higher birds until word got back to Helang in Borneo.

The owl thanked the whale for saving her life and then flew away in a flurry of feathers and embarrassment. She hoped it never got out that she had been rescued by a fish. Ok, a whale. It was not a distinction the owl community would make.

The whale submerged and felt the sting of salt water on the claw scratches. It reminded him of what his sister must have gone through as she felt the harpoon enter her back. Kai had made his decision even as he listened to the birds making plans. He had not bothered to tell them what he intended to do. He did not know whether they would have approved or disapproved. Either way, he didn't care.

The child had run away from her pod. She was alone in a dangerous, human world. Kai did not know London or any other city. But he knew that where there were large human habitats, the air and water were always foul. The animals could not afford for this child to die the way all young ones in the animal world died, who lost their parents too early. The eagle would send word as fast as she could.

But it would take a while for the relay of birds to carry the news across half the globe to Borneo. By that time, it might be too late for the girl – and many creatures of the earth too. He, Kai, was not going to let that happen.

• • •

There was an entrance to a park at the end of the street and Honesty ran towards it. Immediately, she felt better. The light was dappling through the trees. Fields of daffodils, crocuses and tulips extended in every direction. It reminded her of the walk home from school. Honesty remembered how she had marched home every day longing for a television. How could she have been so daft?

Honesty chose a path at random. It led to a big lake surrounded by drooping willows. A few swans were gliding about. Mothers strolled along while their children threw bread to the elegant creatures. The swans drifted over, too stately to show excitement, but not wanting to miss out. Honesty would not have turned down an old crust herself. She sank down onto a park bench, raised her knees to her chest and hugged them tight. This was getting hard.

She was so engrossed in her own hungry thoughts that she did not hear a man sit down at the other end of the bench. And as her eyes were misty with tears, she did not see him.

He asked, 'Is anything the matter?'

She looked around, blinking hard, and saw a smartly

dressed man. He had a packed sandwich for lunch and was holding a folded black umbrella. He wore a round hat with a brim that was slightly funny to Honesty, although she did not know why.

He asked again, 'Is anything the matter?'

Honesty did not answer. Nothing was alright but she was hardly going to tell a stranger in a silly hat.

'I suppose your Mum and the younger ones are feeding the swans?'

She shook her head, gazing at the families feeding the birds enviously.

He unwrapped his sandwich and she could smell the warm bread and grilled vegetables. Her stomach turned over. Her mouth watered. She stole a glance at the food. Organic rye bread. She would swear to it.

He said, 'You look a bit hungry. Would you like half my sandwich?'

Honesty was tempted. But Mum had always been firm on the subject of strangers so she shook her head emphatically and said, 'No.'

And then in case that sounded rude, she said, 'No thank you, I mean. I'm not hungry.'

'Well, you're the hungriest looking 'not hungry' young lady I've ever seen.'

She did not respond so he took a big bite of his sandwich and then pulled a handkerchief out of the breast pocket of his suit and dabbed his mouth and chin. He finished his lunch slowly. Honesty was sure he was one of those people who counted the number of times they chewed their food in their head and did not swallow until they had hit fifty chews. She'd have swallowed that sandwich whole, she knew that for a fact.

Finally, he was done. He got up, went over to a nearby bin, threw away the paper wrapper, walked back to the bench and said, 'If you come with me, I'll take you home and cook you a hot meal.'

Honesty stared at him in surprise. Why would he do that?

The man smiled. His teeth were crooked which did not fit in with his otherwise neat and proper appearance.

'Come along. It will do you good.'

Honesty smiled although she had already decided that the man was a real wacko. Mum always insisted that she be polite to her elders and just because she'd been an awful daughter and run away from home, there was no need to forget her manners. She said, 'Thanks very much.' And then to be on the safe side, 'But I'm just waiting for my Mum.'

'I don't believe you,' said the man, looking around to see if there was anyone within earshot. Honesty looked around too and saw that there wasn't. This was really getting creepy.

'I don't believe you're waiting for anyone. You wouldn't look like that if you were.'

Honesty was very conscious of her grimy clothes and uncombed hair. She stood up and said, trying to keep the nervousness out of her voice, 'I'll be on my way. I think I see my Mum over there.'

He grabbed her arm. He said, 'You can come quietly or I'll drag you kicking and screaming through this park. I'm sure your parents will *pay* very well to get you back!'

'Someone will stop you,' she said, trying to sound confident.

'I'll just say that I'm your father and that you're a wicked, wicked runaway daughter.'

Honesty thought of her own Dad. Large, messy and loving with twinkling eyes and fraying socks.

She *was* wicked to have left her parents. Honesty knew she had made a terrible mistake. She needed to get on a train and go home to her parents and tell them she was sorry and that she would never, ever, ever run away again and then she would prove she was truly regretful by being a model vegetarian, hemp-wearing daughter for the rest of her life.

But to do that she needed to escape.

• • •

Kai turned his face northwards and swam up the North Sea. He dived to avoid being seen by fishing boats and ferries and almost crashed into a man-made tunnel deep under the sea. Kai frowned. Were even the depths of the seas not free from Man's malign influence?

The sea was unpleasant – choppy, cold and dirty. Plastic

rubbish dotted the surface, the flotsam and jetsam of the cruise ships that churned past. Kai knew he was looking for a riverine estuary. He had asked for directions from a seagull. He was not sure how he was going to spot it.

In the end it was not difficult. He sensed a sudden influx of fresh water on his left cheek. He turned towards it and noticed that the sea was noticeably less salty. There was grit and sand swirling in the currents as well, stinging and smarting as he ploughed on.

Kai broke surface to have a look around. Sure enough, he was close to a river mouth. There was a lot of boat traffic. Barges laden with boxes were chugging their way towards the opening and small fishing boats were heading in the opposite direction. There were sandbanks close to the shore. The channel was narrow. Kai would have to be careful not to get beached before he made it up the river to the big city.

The whale was feeling disoriented. His sonar was affected by the thrumming of boat engines, the sound waves magnified under the water. He tried to regain his sense of direction and balance by using only his sight. But it was unnatural for a whale to depend on vision. His eyes were on either side of his great head so they could not work together. He had no depth perception and could not sense how far or near things were. He needed to swim forward, but he could only see things along his sides. He might run into the sharp blades of a boat ahead of him. Kai sent a single fluting note of annoyance through the waters. He had known it would be difficult. But this was ridiculous.

He thought of the young one lost in London without her pod. She was probably just as confused and unhappy as he, Kai, was now. Kai had a moment of doubt. What could one small human girl child do against the determined efforts of so many? How could such a young Animal Talker help them find the Seeds? But this was not the time to hesitate. Not if he was going to swim up this river. This was the time for faith. And strength. He thought of his sister. Her memory would keep him strong.

• • •

The man tightened his grip. Honesty squeaked in pain. She kicked his shin hard. He did not let go but his grasp loosened slightly and she yanked her arm away and started running.

The park was empty. There were no mothers anywhere. No kids. Just the lake and the swans. She ran towards the water, not knowing what she intended. Her thumping heart and thumping feet beat a painful rhythm on the path. She slipped on some gravel and hit the ground and felt the stones graze her palms and her knees. She got back up and kept running. She could not see the man. But she could sense him getting close, hear the pounding on the path behind her. She reached the edge of the lake and looked around. There were people on the far bank. She waved and shouted but, except for a small child who waved back cheerily, they didn't pay any attention.

A couple of the swans drifted closer, hoping for a snack.

She asked urgently, 'Can you help me?'

'What's the matter?' asked the closest bird.

'He's trying to hurt me!' she panted and then started running again. The man was almost upon her but her legs were heavy and her breath was coming in gasps and she had a sharp pain in her chest and her side. Honesty did not know how much longer she could keep going.

The swans flew out of the water – big, white, beautiful birds with strong black and orange beaks. They attacked him, beating the man with powerful wings and pecking at him with their beaks. His hands were in front of his face trying to protect his eyes. He flailed about trying to chase the birds away but he was outnumbered and the swans were airborne. Blood streamed down his face, his clothes were torn and he had trampled on his own hat. He turned and ran away as fast as he could. The swans charged after him, pecking and gouging. Finally, they decided he was not a threat anymore and flew back to Honesty. She was sitting on the ground watching the blood trickle down her shins from her grazed knees. She looked up as the birds settled down next to her.

'Thank you,' she said.

The swans puffed out their chests and leaned towards her with their long graceful necks.

'Always happy to help,' said one of them. 'But you shouldn't be wandering around on your own.'

'I know that now. I'm going home.'

-eighteen-

Kai the humpback whale decided that his best bet was to focus on a single vessel. A slow moving one like a barge. He would try to distinguish the sound of that one barge from the rest and then follow in its wake up the river. That should keep him from getting confused by the other boat engines.

He headed to the river mouth. After watching the barges for a while, he selected a flat-topped barge with a large load of containers that had a curious engine noise. One of its propellers must be dented, Kai guessed. It had a distinct knocking sound that would guide him under the water.

As he had suspected, the river mouth was narrow and deep. It was more than noisy. The channel acted like a tunnel, focussing and amplifying the racket of the engines. Kai was hit by a wall of sound that almost knocked him out. He felt dizzy and sick and had to fight the urge to surface and see where he was. Fortunately, the knocking sound of his barge could be distinguished through the cacophony. Kai homed in on it and kept swimming.

The river water was dank and lifeless. There was not much oxygen. Algae grew thick on rocks and stones and glowed green and slimy. In every crevice, there was human detritus. Rusting metal objects that had once been boats, submerged containers, now a home for fish. Kai thought he might go mad. He tried to keep an image of the open sea and the open skies in his mind to ward off the horror engulfing him.

After a few hours, Kai knew he would have to surface for air and risk being seen. He had no choice. His lungs were burning. He felt light-headed as the carbon dioxide built up in his bloodstream. He remembered, when he and his sister were young whales frolicking across the seven seas, they had dared each other to see who could stay under the longest. He had always won. But he had never stayed beneath the surface for this length of time.

Kai drifted to the surface. This was no time to come shooting out of the water like a reckless dolphin.

He felt a sharp stabbing pain. The water in front of him was clouded with red blood. Kai fought the urge to panic. He sank back down and his vision cleared. He saw that he had been hit by an anchor, thrown over the side by one of the boats. That was just bad luck. Kai shuddered to think what the filthy water would do to the open wound. Still, when he was back in the ocean, the sea salt would clean the cut.

He climbed to the surface again. The water became less opaque. Then he was out in the sunshine, blinking away tears from the brightness. It was a hot day and the light shimmered on the water. He was on a pretty stretch of riverbank. Willow trees hung over the river's edge and the waters swirled in mini-pools under their shade. He could hear the shingle crunching as strollers wandered by. Humans carrying long, thin boats waded in until waist deep in water and climbed in precariously. Kai could hear birdsong although he was not familiar with the calls of birds that lived so far inland. No one noticed the whale. Kai took a deep breath and steeled himself for another plunge into the stinking darkness of the Thames.

He had lost the barge he was following but the traffic had quietened down. Either that or he had gotten used to the barrage of senseless noise. The cut on his head had given him a whale-sized headache but Kai was feeling optimistic. He had come this far against the odds.

The tide had turned and the river was running out to sea. Kai didn't mind. Whales usually swam against the current. He was quite strong enough to run against anything this river could throw at him. But he had not counted on the water getting shallower. As he made his way, Kai could feel his belly scrape against the rocks and rubbish on the riverbed. If he climbed any higher, his dorsal fin would break the surface. The last thing the whale wanted was to be spotted. As far as Kai was concerned, any human, except the Animal Talker he was looking for, was a descendant of Ahab.

Kai had another problem that he could no longer push

to the back of his mind on the slow dangerous journey. How was he going to find the girl? They were both in the big city. They were both far away from home. They were the only two creatures in London who could talk to each other across the species divide. But that did not solve the problem. Kai was a whale in a narrow, shallow river and the girl could be just about anywhere in the city.

First things first. He needed to breathe. Kai came up slowly and found himself in the shadows. He was under a bridge. That was a bit of luck. He was unlikely to be spotted here except by a passing boat. He could see that there were a few tethered along the banks further up, but none appeared to be coming in his direction. He breathed deeply. The air under the bridge stank of diesel fumes. He could hear the rumble of traffic above his head. It really was high time the animals started to push back against Man's domination. He was gratified to be a part of it – except for one small problem. He still had no idea how to find the girl.

• • •

Geram sucked on his blistered finger for a while. Then he walked around the machine on all fours, his long fingers and toes balled into fists. He said, 'What do you think this is?' and held up a long, black rope.

Orang Tua's nostrils flared. 'How am I supposed to know?'

Geram followed the wire, picking it up carefully as he went along.

'Orang Tua, it leads to the lights!'

'So?'

'Maybe that is how they get their power, through this black vine?'

Orang Tua grunted. It was plausible.

Geram was excited. 'We just need to snap this vine!'

He picked up a length with two strong hands and tried to pull it in two. Orang utans are powerful for their size but Geram had no success trying to snap the wire.

'Here, give me that,' said Orang Tua and grabbed the wire from the younger beast. He had no effect on it either.

The two orang utans tried to work together. They grabbed the wire and pulled against each other, a jungle tug of war.

Orang Tua was panting with the effort. The palms of his hands were red and lined with wire cuts. He let go abruptly – without any warning to Geram who was yanking on the wire with all his considerable might. Geram went head over heels backwards. The wire did not snap. But it came undone from the generator. The lights went out abruptly.

• • •

They arrived by helicopter. The chopper, a small busy red machine, picked them up at Fairfax and was hovering right over the tundra, looking for a place to land. The permafrost (permanently frozen layer of soil) meant that water did not drain away from the surface so the tundra was always very wet with a maze of ponds and marshes. The pilot was looking for a dry spot where the men could set up the collapsible, waterproof tents.

'Not that it will do Texic much good, even if I do find the oil down there,' Richard said, as they hovered over the ice.

'Why's that, Dad?' asked Spencer.

'This is all part of an Arctic wildlife refuge. No drilling allowed.'

One of the other men laughed. He said, 'You see that ridge over there,' he pointed at a thin blue line in the horizon. 'Over that ridge is Prudhoe Bay. Plenty of oil work going on over there.'

'But not here,' pointed out Dad to Spencer's relief. His Dad was probably right. Dad knew about this sort of stuff being a grown up and a scientist as well.

The other man said, 'I ain't never seen Mr. Valentine waste his money is all I can say. And flying you around to pick up bits of dirt, if there's no endgame, don't seem like the way he does business.'

They all fell silent contemplating what the man had said.

Spencer was indignant. Drill for oil in a wildlife refuge! He was not at all surprised that Valentine, killer of animals for fun, would do that if he could. But surely no one would let him?

He asked, 'But they can't do that, can they Dad? Drill for oil, I mean. It's not allowed.'

'No, son. It's not allowed.'

'Then why are you looking for oil here if no one is allowed to drill for it?'

There was a silence. Dad must not have heard. Spencer repeated the question loudly over the steady beat of the engine.

Dad said, 'So that everyone can make an informed choice between the various feasible options, son.'

Spencer did not respond. 'Feasible options!' It sounded like adult-speak for doing something really stupid.

• • •

It came to him slowly. Probably because his subconscious was trying to ignore the idea as being too daft to be worth mentioning to the rest of his brain. He, Kai, could not go to the girl. So the girl would have to come to him.

But how was he going to entice a single girl from London's teeming millions to come and see him? There was no way. He would have to entice them all to come. And then perhaps the girl would come too. She would be bound to speak, to show herself. No Animal Talker would pass up the chance to talk to a humpback whale. At least, Kai hoped not.

The thought of drawing attention to himself made his entire huge whale skin crawl. These were people with firesticks and harpoons. These were people who were destroying the natural world. These were the enemy. He was in enemy territory. Unarmed, defenceless and with no quick escape route. But there was nothing for it. He had to tempt the girl to the water. And the time to do it was now.

He flicked his powerful tail and surged out from under the bridge. Glancing back, he could see that he had been sheltering under the most extraordinary structure – a grey stone bridge with blue trimmings and railings and a pretty stone tower at both ends. Even as he looked at it, the middle split open and both halves of the bridge were raised. It was some sort of drawbridge. Kai guessed that this was to allow bigger ships through. Which meant that ships were coming. Which meant he needed to get moving. The last thing he needed was to be harpooned before his job was done.

So, how to make London sit up and take notice? Kai set off at a brisk pace. On the surface he was less distracted by the constant moanings and groanings of the river traffic so it was easier to concentrate on attention seeking. There were a lot of people on the banks but no one spotted him. He sucked in a huge wave of foul-tasting river water and blew it through his spout. That would catch their attention. Except it didn't. This was going to be harder than he thought. He raised his great tail above the surface and crashed it down with a mighty whack. Water sprayed high in the air.

Kai swum with strong, even strokes. Every few hundred

yards he would spout a fountain of water and wave his huge tail to signal the people. It was a beautiful sunshiny afternoon and the warmth on his back helped soothe the whale's fears. The water here was deep so it was more comfortable for the humpback. The cut over his eye from the anchor and the scrapes and bruises along his underside were hurting but not so intensely. If only he could find this girl, talk to her and begin his return journey soon, he would be one very contented whale.

• • •

A small boy, walking with his mother along the river, was talking about dinosaurs. It was all he ever did, so she was used to nodding and exclaiming at the right bits with her mind only partly on the conversation.

'And then,' he said importantly, 'the t-rex chased me but I ran faster and faster, faster even than a t-rex, so it couldn't catch me.'

'Well, that is fast!'

'But then a ptero ... a pterodactyl caught me.'

'Oh dear!'

'It wanted to feed me to its babies.'

His mother wondered where he got this stuff from.

'Did you hear me, Mum? It wanted to feed me to its babies!'

'Yes, dear. What did you do?'

'I fought the pterodactyl!'

'Did you win?'

'Yes, Mum.'

'That's great, darling.'

'Mummy!'

'Yes?'

'There's a whale in the water!'

'Do you mean an ichthyosaurus, honey?' His long-suffering mother knew her dinosaurs too.

'No, Mummy! Over there! It's a whale,' said the boy in an exasperated tone, pointing at the water.

His mother turned to look just as Kai blew a powerful jet of water high in the air. The drops caught the sunlight as they cascaded into the river. It was like a million brightly-coloured jewels rained down on the humpback whale by London Bridge.

After that, Kai did not have to worry about being noticed. The mother grabbed her son and ran to the river bank. She yelled their discovery to everyone they passed. People stared after her in bemusement until they glanced at the river and saw a dorsal fin or a tail or a burst of spray. Then they followed her. Some walked, most ran, all told strangers what they had seen. A ten year old grabbed people by the arm, by the hand or by the coat and dragged them to the water's edge.

The whale cavorted in the sunshine and continued on his way up the Thames. Londoners followed him. They called their friends on their mobiles and tried to reassure them that they knew a whale when they saw one and that they should hurry down to the river as soon as they could if they didn't want to miss seeing it for themselves. A TV crew in a helicopter was soon overhead and images of Kai were beamed all around the world. Reporters interviewed people on the banks about how they had felt when they first saw the whale. People recalled the moon landing and the day JFK was shot.

And as the crowds grew, Kai began to sing.

• • •

Honesty discovered that she had lost all her money. It must have been while she was running away from the man in the bowler hat. She certainly didn't dare go back to look for it. Honesty was hungry, thirsty and longing for a big, forgiving hug from her Mum and Dad. But it wasn't going to be easy to get home. She wandered along aimlessly. There were crowds milling about and Honesty hoped that she blended in. There was no doubt that she was grubbier than most of them. Her knees were grazed. And she had grass stains on the hemp dress. Still, it was better than being alone in the park. Honesty tried to think sensibly. She needed enough money to get a train ticket. She could manage without food. She had read somewhere that the human body could last for weeks without food. It didn't feel like it. Her stomach was an angry, twisted knot of hunger. She couldn't do without water but a few gulps at public toilet taps would keep her from dying of thirst.

Honesty felt hot tears well up in her eyes. She slipped into a shop quickly. The last thing she wanted was to draw attention to herself by bawling on a London street.

She looked around. She was in a television shop. She remembered how she used to stop on the way home from school every day to watch TV. What a fool she had been. Still, this was as good a place as any to try and work out what to do next. Honesty noticed that all the channels were showing the same pictures. She could see the London Eye and Westminster Bridge. What was going on? To her amazement she saw a dorsal fin break surface. It was a whale! Honesty went closer to the TV. She stared at the image of the immense creature. He was singing. She concentrated, trying to make out the faint song of the humpback.

She couldn't believe her ears. The whale sang a song of lost oceans, of bleached corals and of a little girl who could understand the speech of animals. And he begged the girl, if she could hear him, to come to the river and talk to him.

-nineteen-

Honesty stepped out of the shop, uncertain what to do. She set off in the direction of the Thames. She could see the Houses of Parliament in the distance. She hurried towards them. They were almost golden in the sunshine. Big Ben showed the time to be just after three in the afternoon.

She was not the only one heading that way. People were rushing towards the banks of the river, pushing and shoving to try and get to the front. Honesty was elbowed out of the way by a red-faced American tourist in shorts and white socks and then almost knocked over by his equally large, equally red wife, wearing a floral-patterned sun dress and a large straw hat on limp curls.

Honesty was caught on a tide of tourists and swept towards the Thames. She felt hot and squashed. She was worried about falling over and being trampled. The safest option was to go with the flow. Presumably, thought Honesty, people weren't actually jumping into the river so it might be safest up against the railings along the banks. Using her small frame to her advantage, Honesty weaved her way between the people. It was quite easy, really. Many of the others were trying to make it to the river in family groups. They were holding hands and trying to shove their way forward. But there were so many people it was gridlock.

Honesty got to her knees and crawled between the legs of the fat man she had seen earlier. He had come to a standstill. An irresistible force against an immovable object. His wife keeled over, fainting from the heat and the crush. Honesty barely got out from under her in time. She scuttled forward, almost at the river. She could hear people yelling for space and water to revive the woman behind her. She tried to look back but the curtain of people had shut her away from prying eyes.

She got to the gold and black railings. She looked into the water. People were gesturing and pointing and yelling but she could not see anything.

A man said, 'Did you see that?'

Another replied, 'No, no. Where was it? Are you sure?'

A woman in a very smart suit jumped up and down on high heels, teetering and rocking every time she landed, 'I saw it. I saw it. I saw it!'

And then Honesty saw it too.

A shooting plume of spray. A gigantic tail crashing down with a loud splash. The creature disappeared from view under Westminster Bridge and then reappeared, blowing and arcing on the other side. People were pointing and laughing. A grown man with a careful comb over and a bushy moustache burst into tears. Honesty felt hot and cold all over.

There was a whale swimming up the Thames.

• • •

Spencer had never been anywhere as barren as the Arctic tundra. There was not a tree or a bush to be seen in any direction. The ground was covered in hardy, spiky grasses, heathers and moss. There were patches of wildflowers on rocky outcroppings and splashes of orange lichen that broke up the uniformity of the mossy green.

Out to sea he could see the floe edge where sea and ice met. The sea ice was retreating now that it was late spring but it was easy to imagine it forming a solid bridge to an Arctic winter landscape.

It was cold as well. Not quite freezing but cold enough for Spencer to be very glad of his warm jacket, thick gloves and hardy boots.

As he looked out across the ice, scanning the horizon for polar bears, he heard the whirring, throbbing sound of rotors. The helicopter was on its way back. Spencer watched it land. A wall of sound sped across the tundra from the landing aircraft. He saw the men unload the gear as another man disembarked and shook his Dad's hand. Spencer guessed it was the Inuit tribesman that had been hired as a guide. He hurried forward as quickly as his bulky clothes would let him. This was certainly someone who would know where to go to find a polar bear.

• • •

The orang utans knuckled their way around the perimeter of the camp. It did not take them long to track down the second diesel generator from the stink of its fumes.

Geram wrinkled his nose and pointed to the machine with a long, bony finger with tufts of hair between the knuckles.

'There it is,' he whispered and took a step forward.

Orang Tua grabbed him by the arm and yanked him back.

Geram saw what had caught the old beast's attention. There was a single red burning spot next to the generator. It was the lighted end of a cigarette. There was a man on guard.

The apes retreated into the jungle.

'What are we going to do?' asked Geram.

Orang Tua thought hard, his ancient brow furrowed and worried.

'One of us will have to distract him,' he said.

'But he might have a firestick!'

Orang Tua whispered in the darkness, 'I will do it.'

'No, Orang Tua. It should be me. You are too valuable to the tribe.'

Orang Tua shook his head. 'Be that as it may, I am not sure I am strong enough to do what you just did and pull out that black wire.'

Geram greeted this statement with silence. It was the

first time that the old ape had ever admitted a weakness. Geram felt uncertain and afraid. He was not sure whether he was supposed to disagree and reassure Orang Tua – but it was possible that he was right. Geram was strong and had seen far fewer monsoons than Orang Tua.

'Alright,' he said quietly.

They both crept back to the edge of the forest. It did not take Orang Tua long to spot the glowing red cigarette end. He shook his head. What in the world were they doing, the orang utans and the other animals, taking on these man beasts who were tough enough to place lighted twigs in their mouths? Well, there was no turning back. The massed elephants and tigers were waiting and no doubt wondering why it was taking so long for the orang utans to do their part and turn out the lights.

Orang Tua inched forward until he could see the swarthy features of the man. Shadows danced across his face, under the brim of a cloth cap. There was the faint smell of cloves in the air, probably from the cigarette. The man coughed, a hacking sputtering sound. Orang Tua saw him take the lighted twig out of his mouth and spit a giant gob of saliva on the ground. It landed not far from the crouching ape and Orang Tua had to steel himself not to flee.

There was no sign of a firestick. This was not a guard but just someone who couldn't sleep and needed a smoke. But how was he to distract him without waking the whole camp? He could attack him, of course. He would probably win. The human was slight and Orang Tua knew he was much stronger, pound for pound, than a man. But armed reinforcements were bound to turn up. Orang Tua was stumped. He thought angrily to himself that Geram would probably have thought of something by now. He was old and, it seemed, completely out of ideas. Perhaps he should just hand over the task of taking on the men to younger creatures.

The man took the cigarette out of his mouth, dropped it and ground it out with his heel. Then he took a packet out of his shirt pocket, tapped out another cigarette and stuck it between his lips. There was the sudden flare of a flame, shining through a cupped hand, as he lit it. The light reflected off the greasy hair on the man's forehead. Orang Tua had an idea. He crept forward, knuckles to the ground to keep himself low and steady. When he was quite close he climbed a tree, using his hands and feet to grip the trunk securely. He slunk forward on his belly until he was directly over the man. Using one strong arm to anchor himself to the branch, he slid off the tree. His feet, that looked a lot like an extra pair of hands with their long fingers and opposable thumbs, were just an inch or two above the man's head.

Orang Tua grabbed the cap. The man looked up in surprise and saw the orang utan. The ape dangled the hat just over his head and the human made a grab for it. Orang Tua snatched it away in the nick of time. He waved it at the man again, who made another futile grab for it. Orang Tua shinnied down the tree and came within ten paces of the human. Then he put the cap on his own head and cackled loudly. Incensed, the man charged towards the ape. The orang utan turned and dashed into the forest with the human in hot, angry, humiliated pursuit.

Geram watched the pantomime from the sidelines. His respect for the senior ape grew tenfold. Fancy stealing the man's hat! But now, he, Geram, had a job to do. He quickly found the black vine and looked around to make sure no one was watching. He tugged at it hard. The jungle was plunged into an impenetrable darkness.

● ● ●

Things began to go wrong. There were sharp bends in the river and the shores had silted up. The waters were shallower. The river had ceased to flow smoothly too. There were uneven currents and swirling riptides, especially under the bridges. Kai was tired. After a difficult dangerous journey, he had been cavorting wildly to draw attention to himself. He found himself confused and disoriented by the uneasy waters.

Small boats had launched and were following him. The thrumming of their outboard motors, in addition to the yells and cheers of people on the banks, and the steady throbbing of the helicopter engines overhead were making Kai feel very unwell. And there was no sign of the girl. Where was she?

Kai beached. He turned a corner too sharply and ended up on the shingled shore. A full third of his body was out of the river. He flapped his tail frantically, trying to find some leverage to push his great bulk back. It didn't work. The people on the banks fell silent. They didn't know what to do. He could sense them willing him to find his way into the water. But his massive weight, unsupported by the buoyant water, was bearing down on him. He felt as if he was being crushed – as if the hand of fate, offended by his attempts to set his own destiny, was pushing him down against the ground to teach him a lesson.

People scrambled down from the banks. Others dragged their boats onto the shingle and hurried to him. A few jumped over the sides of their vessels and swam up to the whale, keeping out of the way of the flailing tail. They pushed and shoved Kai, trying to get him back into the water. A woman stayed by his head, patting the humpback and soothing him while tears ran down her cheeks. Some of his would-be rescuers were up to their ankles and waists and necks in filthy water, trying with all their puny strength to get the whale back in the Thames.

Kai was getting weaker. He stopped thrashing about with his tail. Each breath was shallow and laboured. Kai called again for the girl. His rescuers were starting to panic. But they were also getting organised. It was easier now that Kai was inert. The men gathered on one side of the grounded creature and pushed in concert. Women and children were pouring water on Kai, using buckets and bottles and even their cupped hands, trying to keep him wet and cool. Some were on their hands and knees trying to dig a trench in the loose sand around the whale to make it easier for him to slide backwards.

Kai gazed at them through his huge, pained eyes and wondered why these people were working so hard to save him when a few days earlier others had killed his sister in cold blood with a harpoon. The thought of his sister was almost the last straw for Kai. Great tears welled up and slid down his cheeks, mingling with the swirling waters of the Thames. He had come so far to honour her memory. To find this runaway girl and beg for her help to find the Seeds. And he had achieved nothing except to discover that humans were complex creatures. He did not understand how they could be good and evil at the same time. Kai sucked as much air as he could into his collapsing lungs and fluted a last frantic call for the child.

'Do you mean me?' asked a small voice.

Kai went completely still. He swivelled a large eye to look around and saw a thin human girl with red hair glowing in the evening sun. The girl was wet and covered in mud. She stared at the whale, while all around people kept digging and watering, pushing and shoving.

Kai breathed, 'You understand me?'

'Yes.'

'You ran away from home?'

Honesty nodded, her eyes wide with shock that this whale should know that.

'We need you!' exclaimed Kai.

Honesty ventured a question in a small voice, 'What do

you mean? How do you know who I am?'

The whale said, 'The beasts have been looking for an Animal Talker.'

'An Animal Talker?'

'A human who can understand us.'

'But how did you know I could do that?'

Kai, the weight of the world pressing down on him, showed a glimmer of amusement, 'A horse told a buzzard who told an owl who told me!'

'I'm just a child. I'm lost and I have no money. What can I do?'

'You must find the Seeds.'

'What do you mean?'

'You must help us creatures,' said Kai writhing impatiently. There was so little time to make this child understand.

Kai was interrupted by a man shouting, 'Hey, girl! Stop bothering the whale.' Someone else grabbed Honesty by the arm and dragged her away.

Kai went ballistic. He found the last of his strength and thrashed about violently. The man who had pulled Honesty away let go in shock and Honesty scrambled back to Kai. The whale calmed down.

A few people gaped at Honesty but she did not notice and neither did Kai.

'How can I save *you*?' asked Honesty in a small, frightened voice.

Kai sighed. 'It's too late for me.'

'Please don't say that!'

'I have been too long out of the water. Even if I could get back in the river, I do not have the strength to reach the sea.'

Honesty knelt down and put her arms around the whale as far as she could reach, trying to communicate her pity and her love for this sea creature so far from its home.

'I am not important,' said Kai. 'But you must listen to me carefully.'

Honesty leaned forward. The whale's voice was growing fainter.

'The animals are trying to save themselves. We are losing our habitat and we are being killed. We are trying to do something about it. But we need help from a human like you.' The whale's breathing was painfully laboured.

'There are Seeds that must be found. I don't know much about it. The Borneo orang utans are in charge. You must contact them.'

'How?' asked Honesty.

'Go back home. Find an eagle – a higher bird. It will carry your message to Borneo.'

The whale's voice was getting fainter and fainter. Honesty leaned forward to try and hear his whispered final words.

'Do you understand me?'

Honesty said, 'Yes!' clearly and loudly. She didn't, of course. She was wet and cold and tired, ankle deep in muddy water, far away from home, trying to comfort a dying whale. Her heart was sore and the grit under her fingernails was smarting. She didn't understand anything but she knew the most important thing she needed to do was help this gigantic beast rest easy.

Neither the whale nor the girl had noticed the increased activity around them. But men were wrapping the whale in rubber and trying to attach floats to his sides. A winch from a crane was being lowered from the road along the river. A large empty barge had drifted into view.

'What are you doing?' shouted Honesty frantically, but she was ignored.

The pontoons were giving Kai a little bit more ballast, so the men could slide the straps around his huge girth. Honesty saw, for the first time, the scratches and welts on the humpback's underside. She noticed the big cut above his eye that was starting to bleed again. She could not understand why this whale had come for her and what she was supposed to do. But she could see how much Kai had suffered.

The winch was attached to the straps enveloping Kai.

A grownup asked, 'But what are you doing?'

One of the men from the rescue services said, 'Trying to get him on that barge to rush him back to sea, ma'am.'

'But if he's afloat, why not just let him go. He could swim back?'

Honesty said in a small voice, 'He's too tired to swim all the way back. He's been out of the water too long.'

The man in charge of the operation said, 'The kid is

right. He doesn't have a hope of making it back on his own. This is his best chance.'

The woman who had asked the first question said, 'This girl managed to quiet the whale. She's been talking to him all the while.'

The rescue worker said to Honesty, 'Do you want to help us get the whale on board?'

Honesty nodded. So while she whispered soothing words to Kai and patted him and stroked him, the whale was winched carefully into the air with his great tail hanging down and carefully transferred onto the deck of the barge. Kai started to struggle feebly as he was moved out of range of Honesty's voice and one of the men shouted, 'Get that girl over here!'

Honesty was hastily bundled into a boat and rushed to the barge. She spoke to Kai and the whale calmed down again.

With a supreme effort, Kai opened his eyes and said, 'You're sure you understand what you must do?'

Honesty said, 'Yes, I won't let you down.'

The whale lowered one eyelid in a conspiratorial wink. 'I'm glad I'm the one that found you,' he whispered. 'They will sing songs of me under the oceans until the stars have fallen from the heavens.'

Outside the water for so long, the humpback was suffocated by his weight. His muscles struggled to give his lungs space. It was too great an effort. The whale's huge body started to spasm. Honesty stroked and patted the whale, trying to calm him. It didn't work. His tail beat frantically against the deck. Kai fought for his life for a few more minutes and then abandoned the effort. He grew tranquil. Honesty knelt down on the deck next to him and looked into his gentle, tired eye. She tried to think of something, of anything that might save this great creature. She willed him to hang on with all the eleven year old strength she had. But it was too late. The end came quickly. The beautiful liquid eyes shut for the last time.

Honesty, the Animal Talker, leaned her aching forehead against the humpback's sandy side. The whale was quiet, still, free. But Honesty's heart thumped against her chest like a drumbeat of pain. She had been alone almost her whole life. A girl who could talk to animals had found neither human nor animal friend. Then for one brief, magical moment she had found an ally, a soul mate. But now Kai the whale was dead, far from his home under the oceans, on a barge under Westminster Bridge.

For a long time there was silence as London mourned its whale.

A tired rescuer wrapped a blanket around Honesty and poured her a cup of hot chocolate from a flask.

He asked gently, 'Where would you like us to take you?'

Honesty looked at him blankly and then remembered the last instructions of the whale.

She said, 'I'd like to go home, please.'

-twenty-

Spencer and the Inuit guide, Ataneq, became firm friends. While the others hovered over their sensitive equipment and pored over maps and rock samples, Spencer and Ataneq wandered across the tundra on a mission to find a polar bear. Once his father saw that the boy was in safe hands, he did not object to their forays, merely warning them to be careful, to keep a satellite phone with them and not to be gone too long.

Ataneq spent hours, as they roamed over the tundra, telling Spencer about the people and creatures of the North. What had seemed a vast featureless plain, soon became a crowded and colourful landscape. Ataneq showed Spencer the Arctic ground squirrel with its inquisitive face and short skimpy tail. They spotted an Arctic fox hurrying along in its spring suit of brown and Ataneq told Spencer that the fox wore a pure white coat in winter. They watched a herd of caribou with forked antlers wander by, grazing intermittently on the rough grasses. Flocks of migratory Arctic geese and ducks winged their way back to the North from their winter break in warmer climates.

But of polar bears, there was no sign. Ataneq told Spencer many tales about the polar bears or 'nanuk' (the Inupiat name for the white bear); how they roamed the ice pack hunting for seals; how the female polar bear would find a den on the Alaskan shore to bear her cubs; and how the polar bears would wait for the ice to return after the long summer months.

'What do you mean, the ice to return?' asked Spencer.

A smile creased the Inuit's weather-beaten face. 'Along the coast the ice retreats during the summer months and refreezes every winter. During summer, some polar bears are stranded on the Alaskan coast. They have to wait until the sea ice refreezes before they can go back to hunting on the ice pack.'

Ataneq's face grew sober. His flat-planed cheeks and narrow eyes were expressionless as he gazed out over the ice.

'Nowadays, the ice takes too long to come back. And the polar bears starve waiting for it.'

'What do you mean?'

'Because of global warming,' the Inuit explained. 'The ice is taking longer to freeze. So the polar bears have to wait longer to go back out to hunt. I've seen them drown because they've tried to swim out to sea for the perennial ice or from ice floe to distant ice floe and it's been too far.'

Spencer shivered. 'Is there anything we can do?' he asked.

'Hope your Dad doesn't find any oil, I guess.'

● ● ●

Just about everyone saw Honesty on TV. Everyone that is, except her Mum and Dad, because they didn't have a television. But the neighbours rushed over with the news. Honesty's parents went back with them to watch the attempted whale rescue on a flat plasma screen. There was no mistaking a tired Honesty stroking the beached humpback. Her mother sobbed in relief and then cried out in panic to see her runaway daughter within a few yards of the thrashing tail of a whale.

Her father was throwing a few things into a bag to head for London when Honesty came home.

No one said anything much. Honesty apologised for running away in a small voice. The rescue crew told her parents how hard she had worked to save the whale. Her parents hugged her and asked no questions. Honesty crawled out of a hot bath, put on her hemp pyjamas, grateful for the rough, warm, comforting fabric and sipped on the hot chocolate her Mum gave her, enjoying the warmth that spread from her stomach to her toes. Honesty expected anger but there was none. Her parents were so grateful to have her back. And they could see from her grimy clothes and tear-stained cheeks that Honesty had had a rough time of it.

School the next day was a different story. Mum said she

didn't have to go in, not till she felt better. But Honesty insisted. It was better to get it over with.

Everyone knew she had run way. Caitlin had filled in the colourful details of her flight. They had all seen her on the television the previous day as the camera crews on board the many news helicopters had beamed her picture live around the world. She was the most un-cool kid in school. And she had run away from home. But now she was a celebrity.

Caitlin summed it up for everyone as she welcomed Honesty back with open arms, hemp clothes and all, 'You're so famous, you might get on Celebrity Big Brother!' she exclaimed, half joking but half hoping it was true.

• • •

The animals attacked the minute the lights went out. The elephants charged the tents and the caravans. Structures collapsed. Vehicles were overturned. Elephants used their trunks to pull tent pins out of the ground. The tents collapsed like deflated balloons.

Humans emerged from the wreckage. They looked dazed and scared. In the darkness they were helpless, unable to see the threat they faced. The animals with their superior night vision had the advantage. The tigers showed no mercy. They flung themselves at the men, going for the jugular. The humans screamed in shock and pain. There was no one to take charge – to organise a response.

The cobras had done their job well. The leaders were lying dead in their bunks.

Then the tide began to turn. Men from the further tents emerged carrying guns. When they saw the animals running amok, some scattered into the surrounding jungle. A few panicked and fired indiscriminately, killing man and beast alike.

The gunshots spooked the captive elephants – they snapped their tethers and stampeded through the camp, crushing everything in their path.

An old bull charged at Gajah and gored him on the shoulder. It took a few paces back, ready to land the killer blow. One of the captives, the female elephant, trumpeted her dismay and attacked the old bull – deflecting him from his target and saving Gajah's life.

A four-wheel drive vehicle burst into flames. The flames licked the other trucks, lying in leaked pools of gasoline. There was a huge explosion. Red and orange flames leapt for the sky. The men with guns had targets they could see by the light of the raging fires.

Harimau the tiger was shot through the heart and died instantly.

Geram screamed with anger. He dropped out of a tree like a stone, onto the back of the man who had shot Harimau. They grappled for the gun. The orang utan was by far the stronger. He wrenched the gun from the man's hand and scampered up a tree. The roars and groans of wounded and dying animals and men grew louder. Geram knew he had to point the firestick. But how to make it hurl death at men? He held up the shotgun and saw the trigger. He pulled it, the gun fired. The bullet grazed his own cheek. Geram fell with a crash to the ground.

The rhino was shouting for the animals to retreat and they were falling back into the jungle. Orang Tua saw Geram lying on the ground. He leapt down to him and grabbed the young ape. Geram was alive. There was blood on his face but he was breathing.

Orang Tua looked around for help. The she-elephant who had rescued Gajah was milling around. She had heard the rhino order a retreat but was torn between her loyalty to the captive elephants and the call of the wild.

Orang Tua roared, 'Help me, please! He's still alive.'

The elephant looked at the ape, ears flapping wildly, eyes rolling with panic. She made up her mind. She curled her powerful trunk around Orang Tua and flung him onto her back. She grabbed Geram in a secure grip and ran for the cover of the trees and darkness.

• • •

The Inuit reached the top of a snowdrift on the sea ice. He motioned with his hand for Spencer to be quiet. The boy crept forward wondering what the guide had seen. It was bound to be something cool. It always was with Ataneq.

It was a polar bear.

A huge bear, more yellow than white against the snow,

with big strong legs and a long snout, was snuffling around the ice.

'What's he doing?' asked Spencer softly. He was so excited he had to bite the inside of his cheek to keep from yelping.

'Hunting!'

'For what?'

'Just watch.'

The polar bear was still sniffing the surface of the ice. Suddenly, he reared up and plunged his front paws hard against the ice. Nothing happened. He did it again, with even more force. There was a sound like a gunshot as the ice cracked under the pressure. The polar bear reached into the water with its great paws and dragged a ringed seal, dark grey with distinctive white rings on its body, out of the hole. The seal struggled, but on land the powerful swimmer was just an ungainly piece of blubber – no match for the powerful bear. Soon, the bear was ripping out large pieces of meat and devouring them hungrily. The snow and ice was stained with red blood – as was the bear's muzzle.

'Awesome!' whispered Spencer.

Two frisky polar bear cubs came bounding out from behind an icy ridge. Their mother moved over to give them a share of the spoils. Spencer couldn't help himself. He squeaked with sheer excitement. The boy covered his mouth with his mittens in horror. He couldn't believe he'd made a sound. Hadn't he just seen what a polar bear could do to a boy-sized seal? He could see from Ataneq's face that he could hardly believe it either. The mother bear looked up in their direction. The Inuit hunter pulled the boy down below the ridge and they lay motionless. Spencer barely dared breathe. He was sure the bear would hear his pounding heart. Ataneq was completely motionless. Spencer hoped he hadn't passed out with fright. He really loved polar bears. But he sure didn't want to be alone with one – or three.

There was a period of intense quiet except for the whistling of a thin, cold wind. Spencer sensed the bear before he saw her. A shadow loomed large and the bear stood over them.

'Lie still,' whispered the Inuit urgently.

Spencer did his best but he was fighting the urge to run for his life as the polar bear sniffed him with a bloody nose.

The two cubs came bounding over the crest. One of them lost its footing and went sliding down the steep side on its rear end. The other one bounced up and down in amusement.

The mother bear said crossly, 'Can you two be careful, please.'

Spencer took his life in his hands.

He sat up and said, 'They're just having some fun!'

Ataneq reacted bravely. He grabbed Spencer, knocked him back to the ground and covered him with his own body, trying to protect the boy from the bear.

The polar bear asked, 'Why is the human behaving so strangely?'

Spencer's voice was muffled as he struggled to crawl out from under his friend. 'I think he's trying to protect me.'

'From what?' asked the bear.

'From you!'

The bear reared up on her hind legs and waved her paws about. 'I could kill you, of course.'

Ataneq looked as if he was going to be sick. His face had turned as white as the snowdrifts.

'But,' the polar bear continued in more conciliatory tones, 'Surely all men know that no polar bear would harm an Animal Talker.'

'I didn't know that, I'm afraid,' said Spencer. 'But I'm really glad to hear it.'

One of the babies came up to Spencer and nuzzled him. Spencer put his arms around the creature and hugged him.

'Why would you not harm me?' he asked.

'We consider you a bear.'

'Oh.'

'There's nothing to stop me eating your friend, of course.'

Spencer was immediately reminded of just how big and strong the beast was. Ataneq was staring at Spencer and the bear in open-mouthed amazement, unaware that it was his status as lunch that was being discussed.

Spencer chose his words carefully.

'The man is like a brother to me. I would be much happier if you did not eat him.'

'It shall be as you wish,' said the polar bear politely. 'We are not that hungry anyway. I have just hunted a seal.'

'I know. I saw,' said Spencer.

The polar bear grinned, baring her long yellow teeth and powerful incisors.

'You are welcome to have a bite.'

'Errr, thanks,' said Spencer. 'But we brought sandwiches.'

It was the most peculiar picnic Spencer had ever attended. They went back to the seal carcass that still reeked of blood.

The bears continued to gorge on the seal. Spencer ate his roast chicken sandwich with pickles. Ataneq picked at his salmon burger but did not seem that hungry.

-twenty one-

It was over and their casualties were high. Three tigers had died including Harimau. Four pygmy elephants had been killed and Gajah was badly wounded. The last two-horned rhino in Borneo had survived unscathed and with him his species for another day. Orang Tua, who had watched him in the thick of the battle charging back and forth, goring any human in his way and hollering instructions the whole time, was astounded that he had not been killed. The cobras and the pythons had not suffered any casualties. Their covert operation had been a success.

The rhino sent Ular the python back at first light to assess the damage to the camp. His report lightened their spirits. The camp was in chaos. Vehicles were upturned. Some were still on fire. The tents and caravans were destroyed. Many men had been killed. The discovery that their leaders had died of snakebite in the night had filled the survivors with a great fear. The humans were a superstitious bunch and Ular heard them insisting to each other that they had been attacked by spirits of the forest who had taken animal forms to fight them.

The men left the camp as soon as dawn broke. Ular watched them go. They did not bother with the bodies of either men or animals. When the python reported back, the beasts returned to the camp and gathered the corpses in a huge pile at the centre of the clearing. The orang utans collected dry wood and leaves and piled it high around the dead. Orang Tua went to a smouldering truck and brought back a lit branch. He carefully placed it at the base of the pyre. They gathered in a circle and watched the flames consume the fallen.

Later that day, Geram recovered consciousness. Even in their sorrow for lost comrades, there was room for laughter at the ape who had shot himself with a firestick.

Orang Tua said in his most pompous voice, 'Let that be a lesson to you, young fellow. The weapons of Man are not for us.'

This had caused them all to laugh even harder.

It was the rhino who sobered them.

His words were like a cold trickle of water dripping off a leaf onto the back of their necks. 'One down, many camps to go. That was just a skirmish. The real war begins now.'

• • •

Spencer met the polar bear family everyday. Ataneq was sworn to secrecy. He agreed not to tell what he had seen partly, Spencer suspected, because he did not expect to be believed. The Inuit guide treated Spencer with a mixture of respect and awe. It was unbelievable to him that Spencer could communicate with the polar bears. But he had seen it with his own eyes. Spencer had tamed a fully grown female just by speaking to her.

The boy objected to the word 'tamed'.

'They're not tame, Ataneq. They're as wild as they've ever been. But they have some ancient custom that they do not kill Animal Talkers.'

'But that means there are others like you!'

'Not for a long time. Mother bear was saying that, until I turned up, there hadn't been a man bear in living memory.'

'Man bear?'

'That's what they call people like me,' said Spencer sheepish, but proud.

The polar bears took him for long walks across the ice. The mother would talk to Spencer and the cubs would play rough and tumble games with him. They would slide down snowdrifts on their rears, see how far they could skate across the ice (the cubs always won, they had much better balance on all fours) and leap across crevasses, daring each other to cross the widest cracks. It was tremendous fun. And when he apologised to mother bear for taking her cubs away from their lessons in survival, she had laughed and said that games were all part of learning the tricks of the ice. Spencer remembered his days in school, sitting in a chair while the teacher droned on about geometry. The polar bears certainly knew a lot more about teaching kids than the New York school board.

The polar bear explained how tough things were getting out on the ice.

'That seal was my first meal in a long time,' she said. 'I can survive but I'm worried for the cubs. They must build up their fat stores. Otherwise, they won't make it through the next winter.'

Spencer watched the two cubs pound the ice to find a seal. They had no luck and decided to practice standing on their heads instead, screeching with laughter as they rolled over.

'This pair do seem particularly silly,' mother bear said lovingly.

'Did you have other litters then?' asked Spencer politely.

'Yes, a pair of cubs three springs ago. But they did not survive.'

Spencer was silent. What could he possibly say?

Mother bear said matter of factly, 'I tried so hard. But the ice did not reach the denning grounds until the days had grown short and the sun distant. There was no food on land – the grizzlies had taken it all. By the time the ice returned, there was not enough time to prepare for the endless night. I survived, but the cubs died on the evening of the coldest day.'

'Will it be better this year?' asked Spencer in a small voice, wondering whether he could try hoarding sandwiches for the bear cubs.

'I hope so,' she said. 'But I wish I knew why the ice is turning against the white bear. Chunks break off the glaciers and the ice mountains and float away to sea. Bears are stranded on icebergs. The sea ice comes to shore later and later. It turns to water earlier. We bears have always respected the ice.' The polar bear looked at Spencer sadly. 'Can you tell me, man bear, why the world is changing?'

Spencer knew, of course. Which eleven year old didn't? He knew that the burning of fossil fuels was warming the planet. He knew the rainforests that sucked up carbon dioxide were being destroyed. His own Dad was looking for oil in an Arctic refuge. Spencer knew all the answers but he just shook his head mutely. He was too ashamed to explain.

$$\bullet \bullet \bullet$$

Mr. Valentine was in a rage. He did not like bad news.

The wolf was not afraid of Valentine's tantrums. But he retreated to a corner of the room. He had once been hit by a flying shard of glass when Valentine flung a crystal tumbler full of whisky at a wall. The glass had cut and the whisky had stung. The wolf was not afraid, but he was prudent.

It was news of the destruction of the plantation camp in Borneo that had so annoyed Valentine. He had deadlines to meet. Oil palm saplings to plant. This was not the time for an entire camp to abandon the job because they had come across some wildlife. It was a jungle – what did they expect to see, rabbits? Anyway, the tale that had filtered up from the camp was absurd. According to the workers who survived, they had been attacked by spirit creatures of the forest. The spirits had adopted the guise of animals and torn the camp apart. Mr. Bent had sent word that it would not be possible to reopen the camp – no one was prepared to work there, not for any amount of money.

Mr. Valentine scowled and looked around for something to throw. There wasn't anything. A mobile phone rang. There was a delicate lull in proceedings while he debated whether to hurl the phone at the wall or answer it. He picked up the phone and flicked it open with a manicured finger nail.

'Valentine,' he said curtly.

It was Mr. Bent at the other end. His gravelly voice was unmistakable.

'I've been looking into it – you know, the incident at the camp in Borneo.'

'And?' asked Valentine irritably.

'And … you're not going to believe this, but my foreman insists it was a coordinated attack.'

'By one of our competitors?'

'No,' there was a sudden silence on the line and then Mr. Bent continued in a low tone, 'By the animals!'

'What?' Valentine's exclamation was like a bullet shot. Tarzan's eyes rolled and his ears flattened against his head.

'What do you mean, by the animals?'

'Apparently, senior crew members were killed in their bunks before the attack started, bitten by cobras while they slept. My foreman only survived because he was … chasing an orang utan who had stolen his hat. Tigers and elephants spearheaded the actual attack.'

'Have you been drinking?' asked Valentine roughly.

'Look, I know it sounds ridiculous but you asked me to investigate and this is what I found out!'

'Ok, why didn't they just shoot the animals? Presumably they've all got guns.'

'The lights were sabotaged.'

A broad smile spread slowly across Valentine's face, sending waves of flesh rippling outwards. The wolf came closer – he was curious. Valentine said, 'Well then, I will tell you exactly what to do.'

• • •

Helang's news was good. There was a confirmed sighting of an Animal Talker, a human girl who could talk with the beasts. A whale had carried word of their quest to her. The information was greeted with excitement and relief. Orang utans performed excited acrobatics across the treetops. The snakes did a complicated swaying dance to show their pleasure. The pygmy elephants trumpeted in unison. The tiger who had taken over leadership from Harimau, a much more reasonable creature called Kucing, purred loudly – the deep sound thrumming through the undergrowth. Helang flew a small neat circle and then returned to her branch to continue her tale, she was so thrilled by her own news. Only the rhino was impervious. He listened to Helang's story quietly, nodding only once in acknowledgement, when he heard of the whale's sacrifice.

He said in his penetrating voice, 'We need a plan. This is the endgame.'

The others fell silent one by one until the only sounds were the shrieks of the cicadas and the mournful bass of a lonely bullfrog.

'What do we want from this child?' the rhino asked. He answered his own question. 'We need her to help us find the Seeds. Without the Seeds, all our sacrifice in battling the humans will just hasten our extinction.'

'What should we do?' asked Gajah in a pained voice. His shoulder wound was not healing well. The others were worried about him.

'We must share with her everything that our Collective Memory has told us about the Seeds.'

'But how do we know we can trussst her?' hissed Ular.

'We don't know. We *can't* know.'

Geram, who had become a less aggressive and more thoughtful creature since shooting himself in the face, said, 'But if she turns against us, if she sides with her own kind ... we would have told her the location of our only hope. She could destroy the Seeds ... and us.'

The rhino blinked short-sightedly at the orang utan.

'You are right, of course.'

'Then why give them to her?' asked Kucing.

'Let me finish!' snapped the rhino irritably. He longed for Harimau at moments like this. Kucing was much easier to deal with but there was no doubt she was not the brightest.

'We beasts have not been able to understand the clues in our Collective Memory. We cannot do it on our own. I believe it is a risk we have to take. We must trust the girl.'

He looked around at the animals. The scent of fear was sharp and rancid.

'We can, of course, just go down fighting. That is all I have left in my future. And if we do not try for the Seeds – that is all you have as well.'

Kucing rumbled, 'But…,' she paused, uncertain of what to say next that would best express her doubts.

Orang Tua, who had been strangely quiet during the debate, spoke. 'I agree with the rhino. We must save our forests or die trying. We must ask the Animal Talker for help.'

There were grunts, growls and reluctant hisses of approval. Orang Tua had timed his intervention well. He himself had no doubt that the girl was their only hope. But by appearing to have been convinced by the rhino's words, he had swayed the rest.

The rhino said, 'Are we all agreed then?'

There were nods all round.

'Ok, Helang, you know what to do. Send someone

reliable to speak to the girl. Explain the clues of our Collective Memory. If she can identify the location, send word back to us. If she wants to try and recover the Seeds, we do not object.'

Geram said, 'She is young. She might not be able to do much.'

'If that is the case, we will have to think of something else. But we need to know where the Seeds are first. And for that, we need this child.'

He continued, looking seriously at Helang, 'And one more thing ... tell your messenger – not one word of our fight to buy time.'

Helang looked confused, 'What do you mean?'

'We must not tell this child that we are attacking her people ... her species. She may refuse to help.'

'Can it be right to lie to the Animal Talker?' asked Gajah.

'Not lie ... omit the full truth!'

The rescued she-elephant said snidely, 'You sound almost *human* now.'

The rhino looked at her worriedly, 'You may be right ... but she is the only Animal Talker we've found. We cannot afford to take the chance.'

-twenty two-

Honesty woke up and sat bolt upright in her bed. It was dark. She could not see anything. But she had definitely heard something. There it was again, a sharp, urgent rat-tat-tat at the window. Honesty huddled under her blankets and wondered what it could be. A branch? Knocking against the glass? But the apple tree outside her window would have had to have grown a lot that day to reach her window. Again, she heard the tapping sound. Louder this time. At this rate, the glass would break and whatever it was would get in.

Honesty took her courage in her hands and got out of bed. Her bare feet made no sound as she padded towards the window. There was nothing there. No branch tapping. Nothing. Perhaps she had dreamt it. She turned to go back to bed. There it was again – rat tat tat. Honesty whirled around and saw two large golden eyes peering into the bedroom.

In the split second before she could scream her lungs out, Honesty realised it was an owl. A large barn owl perched on the window sill, peering in with luminous eyes and rapping on the window with its beak.

Her racing heart slowed down to a more manageable speed. Honesty raised the window sash. The owl hopped in and flew around the room in a silent rush of feathers. Satisfied that the room was safe and there were no pet cats lurking, the owl settled on the back of a chair.

'Hoo, who?' the owl hooted.

Honesty gawped at the bird.

'Who, who?' the owl repeated more urgently.

Honesty realised with a start that the owl was asking her who she was.

'Err ... Honesty,' she said. 'Honesty Smith.'

The owl nodded her big head with the sleek feathers and said, 'You understand me? You understand owl? Toowittoowoo?'

'Yes, I do!' She had to stop herself from saying 'do-hoo-hoo'. The owl would probably think she was laughing at her if she copied her accent.

The owl let out a long whistling hoot of relief. 'I am so glad I've found you!'

'I'm glad too,' said Honesty, remembering her manners. 'But why were you looking for me?'

'You remember the whale?' asked the owl.

'Of course I do!' said Honesty, indignant at the suggestion that she could forget her marine mammal friend.

The owl swivelled her head from side to side. 'He was my friend too-hoo. He saved my life once.'

There was a temporary silence while Honesty waited for an explanation of the circumstances that could possibly have led to a humpback whale saving the life of a barn owl.

The owl changed the subject. 'The whale told you that we needed you-hoo-hoo?'

She said, 'Yes, he did. He told me to come back home and wait for more news. But I didn't understand what it was he thought I could do.'

'Do-hoo-hoo? You can save the rainforests!'

The owl buried her head in her chest and groomed her soft, downy feathers. Honesty waited patiently, pulling on a dressing gown against the chill and sitting on the edge of her bed.

The owl said, 'It is difficult to explain.'

'Just try,' urged Honesty.

The owl peered at her with yellow eyes as if trying to see into her heart.

'Things are bad in the animal world,' said the owl quietly.

'What do you mean?'

'The forests are being cut down, the weather is changing, many creatures are on the brink of extinction.'

Honesty nodded. She was not her parents' daughter for nothing. She knew all this stuff. That was why their car ran on cow poo.

The owl continued, 'We have decided to push back. To try and stop Man destroying our world.'

'How?'

'Not how! Who-hoo-hoo? It is you who can help us!'

'But what can I do?'

The owl paused and seemed to be debating whether to continue her story.

'There are Seeds from the earliest days. Seeds that will grow into forests in days and weeks. Seeds that will regenerate the rainforests and create homes for the animals again.'

'That's great!' exclaimed Honesty. 'But what has this to do with me?'

'We need your help to find the Seeds.'

'Me? But I have no idea where they might be.'

'The beasts have clues from our Collective Memory …'

'What's that?' Honesty interrupted the bird.

The owl shrugged, a delicate, feathery gesture. 'We do not really know how it works. But Higher Beasts have memories of things that happened long ago – going back many, many generations. That is how we know about the first Seeds – hidden away for an emergency like we face now.'

'So where are the Seeds?'

The owl hooted in exasperation. 'We don't know. The memories of the Seeds are old and faded.'

Honesty waited for more.

'I am here to tell you the clues and ask for your help in finding them.'

'Me? What can I do?'

'I just told you-hoo,' said the owl impatiently, 'help us

find the Seeds! You are our last hope.'

'Yes, but … ,' Honesty stopped, struggling to find the words. Honesty couldn't believe what the owl was saying. What were the animals thinking? If she was their last hope, the orang utans and the rest were doomed. She'd never been any good at anything except English – that was no training for finding Seeds and saving the rainforests.

She tried to explain, 'Why me? I'm just a child. And I'm not good at anything. You can ask anyone, they'll tell you the same thing.'

'You're the only Animal Talker we've found,' said the owl.

Honesty remembered Kai. The whale had crossed the oceans looking for her. He had sacrificed his life to find an Animal Talker. Honesty closed her eyes. She remembered his song and the moment in the television shop when she had realised that Kai was looking for her. She remembered her friend, beached and bruised but proud. He had believed that she could do it. Honesty took a deep breath.

She said, 'I'll do my best. For Kai.'

The owl was silent. Her golden eyes were glistening. Honesty guessed that she too was remembering the whale and what he had done. There was no time to waste though. There were Seeds to find. Honesty hugged her knees and leaned forward.

She said, 'Tell me the clues, then!'

'The Seeds are located where the ground is covered in a white cold blanket. Waves of light fill the skies …'

'Wait a moment,' said Honesty anxiously. 'I'd better write this down.'

She rummaged for a pencil and a notepad (recycled paper) and wrote down the clues.

When the owl had finished she looked down at her notes.

- *White cold blanket on ground*
- *Waves of light in sky*
- *White bears roam*
- *A sea unicorn guards*
- *Five fingers beckon through the gates*
- *Green mountain*

The owl asked hopefully, 'Can you help us? Do you understand the clues?'

Honesty shook her head ruefully, 'No, but I can do some research tomorrow. At the school library.'

The owl said, 'Then I will return tomorrow night and every night until you tell me we have found the Seeds or there is no hope!'

Without another word she flew straight out of the window in a silent rush of feathers.

• • •

'You are quite sure?' Valentine snapped.

'Yes sir!'

'At current oil prices, that should be quite economical to

extract – it's a bigger reserve than I expected.'

'But there are difficulties, sir.'

'Tell me.'

'Well, firstly the oil is in an Arctic wildlife refuge – along the northern coastal plains of Alaska and right up to the foothills of the Brookes Range. It will be difficult to get permission to extract it.'

'Leave that to me,' said Valentine abruptly. 'What else?'

'The oil is in small pockets. The total volume is large as you say … but the footprint to get it out of so many different spots will be very damaging to the environment – different drilling zones, pipelines, potential tanker spills, refineries – it will affect the whole ecology. I doubt if wildlife like the musk ox, caribou and polar bear will survive the disruption.'

'I don't pay you to make policy. I pay you to find oil.'

'Yes, Mr. Valentine.'

Valentine snapped his phone shut and threw the wolf a biscuit.

'Tarzan, we're almost there,' he said and chuckled.

At the other end, Spencer's Dad watched his son walk back towards the base with his Inuit friend. He knew that Spencer would not be pleased with his day's work.

Spencer was yelling something. He strained to hear but the wind was snatching the boy's words and scattering them across the coastal plains.

Spencer was almost at the camp before his father could make out his words, 'Dad, Dad! I saw a musk ox today. It was huge and shaggy and it had curling horns and it was just amazing!'

'That's wonderful, son. It really is.'

Spencer gave his father a hug. 'This is the most wonderful place on earth, Dad. Thanks so much for bringing me here!'

• • •

Honesty got out of bed the next morning, heavy-eyed but excited. At first, she was not convinced that any of it had really happened. Had she really spoken to an owl about first Seeds that could reforest the jungles of Borneo? But then she found her note with the clues and spotted the rents in the chair fabric from the owl's sharp talons. It had really happened.

And she, Honesty, could help the animals find the Seeds. There *was* a reason that she understood the animals, was an Animal Talker. It was so that she could help save them! She remembered Kai the whale again and felt a wave of panic. She could not bear it if he had died in vain because she was not up to the job.

All the way to school she pondered her clues. The first one was quite straightforward. An orang utan from a Borneo rainforest might not recognise a cold, white blanket but Honesty was convinced it meant snow on the ground. And the white bear could be a polar bear, she supposed. But waves of light and sea unicorns? Honesty was stumped.

There was only one thing to do. Honesty waited on tenterhooks for break time and was twice told off for not concentrating. That wasn't right, of course. She was concentrating hard, just not on her lessons. The minute the bell rang, she dashed out of class to the computer library. She needed to Google her clues.

Honesty searched 'waves of light' first and got nothing useful at all. The results, over a million, were about the frequencies of light waves. Honesty didn't understand a word. Next she tried 'sea unicorn'. She had better luck with that. There was actually a creature called a narwhal, a sort of whale or porpoise with a long spiral horn on its forehead. And it was also known as a sea unicorn. Honesty stared at the pictures in amazement. What an extraordinary beast. She read on and discovered that the narwhal was found mostly in the waters of the Arctic Ocean.

Honesty sat back in her chair. It did seem that, taken together with the white bear, which Honesty was convinced was a polar bear, the Seeds were somewhere very North. That would also explain the blanket of snow and the bone-chilling cold described by the orang utans and gorillas.

Googling 'green mountain' was a complete failure. It seemed to be a brand name for everything from screwdrivers to corn flakes. Honesty looked at the wall clock. It was almost time to go home. She dashed to the school library and asked for a book on the Arctic. She could continue researching at home. Honesty selected a glossy book with a depressed-looking polar bear on the cover.

• • •

Spencer was saying goodbye to a depressed-looking polar bear. It was time to get back to the research camp and Mum. He did not know when they would be back out on the ice. Dad was being evasive. In fact, he had been quiet and moody for days. Spencer, having a lark roaming the tundra with his polar bear friends, had not really bothered about it. Probably Dad was struggling to find the oil. Spencer couldn't care less about that.

Spencer hugged the big polar bear, burying his face in the bear's thick fur.

'I'll come and look for you the minute we get back here,' he said.

'We will always be pleased to see you, man bear.'

The two young cubs frolicked around Spencer. One of them reared up and put his paws on the slender boy's shoulders, knocking him over. They rolled around on the ground, laughing and giggling. Spencer dragged himself to his feet, gave them both a hug, raised his hand in farewell to their mother and trudged off towards the camp with his Inuit friend. His heart was heavy. He knew that the polar bears might not survive. But there was nothing he could do except hope.

• • •

That night, Honesty sat in bed with the pillows piled

up high to support her back, her blankets tucked around her legs and the heavy book on the Arctic balanced against her knees. She was turning the pages, reading every word and scrutinising every picture. She was determined not to miss any hint of a clue. The window was open for the owl's promised visit and every now and then a cool gust of wind would make the hair on Honesty's arms stand to attention. She rubbed her hands along her arms to warm them up and felt the roughness of goose bumps.

So far, there was nothing on her other clues, the 'waves of light' or the 'green mountain', let alone any 'gates' or 'fingers'.

She heard a soft hooting and looked up. The owl was on the window ledge, politely waiting to be invited in. Honesty turned a page and beckoned to the owl.

The bird flew in and perched on the end of the bed.

'Any luck?' she asked.

'A little bit,' said Honesty. 'I'm sure that the Seeds are somewhere north of the Arctic Circle. And the 'sea unicorn' might well be a narwhal. But some of the other clues like the 'waves of light' are a mystery.'

Honesty glanced down at the new page in front of her. She was wrong. On the double page were undulating multi-coloured sheets of light. They filled the sky in mysterious waves of intense colour over the shadowy outline of spruce trees and a blue-black lake.

'The aurora borealis.'

'I beg your pardon?'

'The aurora borealis – the northern lights!'

The bird looked peeved. 'I have no idea what you are talking about, young lady.'

She flew over, balanced on Honesty's knees and craned her head to look down at the book.

Whooping with excitement, the owl spread her wings, flew to the ceiling, bumped her head and settled back on Honesty's knees, gripping her so tightly through her pyjamas she yelped with pain.

'The waves of light,' she hooted. 'The waves of light!'

-twenty three-

Oil prices hit a new high on global markets. Unrest in the Middle East, a storm in the Gulf of Mexico and a coup in a major African oil nation conspired to drive up prices. Within days, the cost of petrol at the pumps had doubled. Angry commuters and irate drivers were interviewed on television waving their fists at gas station attendants and demanding that the Government 'do something'.

Valentine chuckled, rubbed his small, fat hands together in glee and sent his best-looking spokesperson – tall, fit, with a full head of dark hair and honest brown eyes – to tell the nation that the oil reserves in Alaska's North Shore were three times as much as had been previously thought and perfectly commercially viable to extract at current prices. 'And,' the handsome spokesman continued, looking directly into the cameras, 'modern extraction methods mean that the pristine beauty of our Alaskan wilderness will be preserved for generations, even as we extract every last drop of oil!' He looked down, apparently overcome with the emotion of the moment.

Elliot Valentine crooked a finger at an aide. 'Double that man's salary,' he said happily.

It did not take long after that. Valentine spent the day on the telephone with politicians who owed him favours. The public were clamouring for cheap gas. The environmentalists were drowned out by scientists on Valentine's payroll scoffing at the idea that there might be harm to wildlife. And over and over again, the cable TV channels played that segment of the spokesman choking up with emotion at the prospect of cheap oil and happy polar bears.

Valentine's company was soon licenced to extract commercial oil and gas from Alaska's wildlife refuges.

Mr. Valentine popped open a bottle of very expensive champagne, poured a glass for himself and tipped some into Tarzan's water bowl. It was time to celebrate.

• • •

Honesty was back at the library. She felt that she was close to a breakthrough. She had northern lights, narwhals and polar bears – she just needed to figure out what in the world, or to be more precise, where in the world, the 'green mountain' and the 'fingers beckoning through the gates' were. She had researched the northern lights and been disappointed that they occurred across much of the Arctic Circle, from Alaska, across Canada to northern Europe. That was hardly narrowing the search. She printed out a map of the Arctic and shaded in the areas where polar bears roamed, where narwhals had been spotted and the aurora borealis appeared. It was no use. It was far too big an area.

She hunted through the library, asked the librarian, pestered her teachers and Googled every combination she could think of but there was no breakthrough.

As she trudged home that day, she noticed that the television screens in the high street shops were showing polar bears roaming the ice. Honesty had not stopped to watch TV on the way home from school since her London adventure. But today she walked into the shop on an impulse, curious to know what was being said about the polar bears. It was not good news. Drilling was to commence for oil in an Arctic wildlife refuge in Alaska. Scientists who weren't on Valentine's payroll were convinced it would seriously affect the polar bears and other wildlife in that region. The cameras focussed on a mother bear and a couple of joyful youngsters and faded to black. One did not have to be David Attenborough, Honesty thought, to know what the future held for them.

● ● ●

The animals in the rainforests of Borneo were in two minds whether to continue their attacks. The girl had been found. Perhaps the Seeds would be found soon too. Should they stop and wait and hope? Or keep fighting on the basis that every tree saved was a precious bit of habitat for the few remaining Higher Beasts?

The rhino summoned the Council. One by one they arrived in the clearing in the half-darkness of the evening. A thick covering of mist hung over the gathering. The air was damp and Orang Tua could feel his bones ache with the pain that heralded the coming of the rains.

'Are we all here?' asked the rhino. He sniffed the air and answered his own question, 'Kucing is not here yet.'

He waited, impatiently pawing the ground, and then snapped, 'She's late. We'll start without her.'

Ular reported that work at the camp they had attacked had not resumed. The superstitious fallout from the workers was a huge bonus.

The rhino was insistent, 'If they are too afraid to come back once we attack them, we could clear humans out of Borneo ourselves!'

Orang Tua snapped, 'You are being naïve. We scared them away from one camp. If we attack the rest, they will have no choice but to fight back. They will never leave of their own accord.'

'But what if no one will work in the jungle?' asked Gajah, raising his trunk in a question mark.

'They will find a way. Bribe, threaten, bully – the humans will find a way,' argued Orang Tua.

'I agree with the rhino,' said the King Cobra. 'We should fight on.'

'Well, I don't!' shouted Orang Tua angrily.

'All creatures in the jungle know that snakes speak with forked tongues,' said the she-elephant.

The cobra reared up and flared its hood in anger. 'How dare you insssult me,' she hissed. 'You, who have ssslaved for the humans while we fought them. Even now you do their will!'

Geram stepped forward hurriedly, getting between the angry snake and the she-elephant. 'Stop it everyone. No one doubts the honesty of your advice, Cobra.' He turned to the elephant, 'And no one doubts the freedom of your views. We are all in this together.'

The she-elephant nodded sullenly. She was struggling to adapt to the wild after a lifetime of captivity. It was making her nervous and short-tempered.

The snake too, subsided. He knew his worth to the fight. The animals would not have succeeded in their first attack without the cobras.

The rhino said enthusiastically, 'If we attack all the major camps simultaneously, we could drive the humans out of Borneo. I am sure of it.' He continued, 'And we need not even take heavy casualties. We were unlucky the last time to start a fire so the humans could see to use their firesticks accurately.'

'How come Geram couldn't see what he was doing then?' squawked Helang to loud guffaws from all the animals. All, that is, except Geram who rubbed the puckered scar on his face ruefully.

Orang Tua winked at the bird. The joke had reduced the

tension among the animals.

'If we have the jungle to ourselves, even for a few rains, many of our species will recover from the brink of extinction,' the rhino continued persuasively. 'We may not even need the Seeds!'

Orang Tua scratched a flea in his armpit. The rhino was convincing. But he was afraid that the creature was getting reckless. Desperate for revenge, with a lot less to lose than the rest, was his judgement clouded?

A rasping voice said from the sidelines, 'I am here for the tigers. We apologise for being late.'

The rhino looked at the lithe, young tiger in surprise. 'Where's Kucing?' he asked.

'Dead.'

'Dead? What do you mean? How?' The animals hissed and chattered their shock.

'Shot by a poacher,' the tiger said. 'I found her. She had been skinned – and …' he bowed his head, 'her eyes and claws were missing.'

There was a horrified silence.

'We are sorry,' said Orang Tua. 'She will be missed.'

The tiger nodded. 'She was my mother. I am here to take her place.'

-twenty four-

'The five peaks of the Arrigetch mountains do look like beckoning fingers, I suppose,' said Honesty doubtfully.

The owl looked unconvinced.

"Arrigetch' means 'fingers of a hand outstretched'. And the peaks, they're part of the Brookes Range, *are* sometimes known as the gates of the Arctic.'

The owl's silent scepticism spoke louder than words.

It had taken Honesty weeks of furious research following up on obscure references, while the owl got more and more depressed, to track down anything that looked a tiny bit hopeful. She had printed out the information and brought it home to the owl. They stared at the five peaks again – towering snow-capped mountains wreathed in clouds and reaching the heavens.

'But none of them are green,' protested the owl. 'More like smoky blue.'

'The lower parts, below the snow line, must have trees and things,' guessed Honesty.

'That hardly makes any of the peaks a 'green mountain''

justifying a Collective Memory that had survived since before owls evolved,' the owl pointed out crossly.

But Honesty was sure she was getting closer – she had found her beckoning fingers and they were calling her to Alaska.

'Even if you're right, and the Seeds are in Alaska – how are you going to get there?'

It was a good question from the owl. Honesty thought hard. It was late autumn. Soon the cold and snow and ice would make any hunt for the Seeds impossible till the following spring. That might be too late for the animals of Borneo who had asked for her help. And it might be too late for the wilderness where the Seeds were hidden if the oil companies had started drilling by then. She, Honesty, had to get to Alaska. But she didn't have a clue how.

'I could try and run away again,' suggested Honesty hesitantly. 'I have a passport. I have no idea why, London's the furthest I've ever been from home.'

The owl did not know what a passport was and did not care.

'You-hoo were lucky the last time. There might not be whales around to save your hide if you run away again.'

Besides, thought Honesty, it would be difficult to steal enough money for a plane ticket. And she didn't want to do that to her parents again. Perhaps the best thing to do was the most obvious. She would ask her parents.

That evening, at the dinner table, she tried. 'Mum, I would love to see the aurora borealis!'

'What's that, Honey?'

'The northern lights, Mum. Those waves of light caused,' she paused to remember what she had read, 'by electromagnetic fields near the Poles.'

'I've seen pictures,' said Jane. 'It is beautiful, darling.'

'It would be just great to go to Alaska and see it, don't you think?'

'Yes, it would, Honesty. But you know I don't approve of flying because it's so polluting!'

'But we could set off our carbon emissions? You know, plant some trees.'

'I suppose so,' Mum said doubtfully.

They ate the rest of their dinner in silence.

That night, Jane told her husband about Honesty's sudden desire to visit Alaska.

Samuel looked at her in surprise. 'You don't think we should go, do you?'

'I wondered.'

'But why?'

'She's a good girl.'

'We can't indulge every whim of Honesty's because she ran away once.'

Honesty's Dad was a perceptive man. He knew his wife was still labouring under a terrible guilt that her only child had been unhappy enough to run away from home.

Jane said, 'She's been as good as gold since she got back. And we haven't changed anything for her. Remember, we discussed getting a TV but we never did.'

'She didn't want one,' Sam reminded her.

'Well, she's just been trying so hard, hasn't she, to make us proud.' Jane fell silent for a moment and then continued, 'And this Alaska thing's not a flash in the pan. She's had her nose buried in books about the Arctic for weeks. She might get really interested in a career in something we care about. You know, like wildlife conservation, if we show her some of these wonders close up.'

Honesty's father looked at his wife in surprise. 'You really mean it, don't you? You want to take her?'

'Yes,' said Jane firmly. 'I think she deserves it. And we can set off our carbon emissions. Plant some trees.'

'I'm not really sure,' sighed her Dad.

Honesty's mother, arguing more with herself than her husband, said, 'I know it seems indulgent. But goodness knows that's not something we've been particularly guilty of her whole life. She's never been on a holiday. She's only ever worn home-made clothes. We've never bought her a present in a shop or a meal in a restaurant.'

'Yes, I know she's not had the easiest time. But we both agreed that it was the only way we could look her in the eye as an adult and say we did our best for her.'

'But it's been so tough ...'

'Jane, it's not been that bad. Honesty's a great kid. She's smart. She's healthy and happy too.'

'Happy? Sam, she ran away from home!'

Honesty's father put up a hand, as if to ward off the hard truth of that last statement. He said, 'Ok. If that's what you really want to do. I need to stay here with the farm. But you and Honesty go. It will be fun!' he added, grinning at his wife who was pirouetting around the room in excitement.

Honesty could not believe her ears the next morning. She gaped at her Mum, 'We can go … to Alaska?'

'Yes, your father and I discussed it. We can go to Alaska. Just you and me though. Dad has to mind the farm.'

'But … but why?'

'Because you've been wonderful since you got back and your Dad and I just want you to be happy.'

Honesty flung her arms around her mother. 'I *am* happy, Mum. This is the most fantastic thing that has happened to me ever!'

● ● ●

The fate of Kucing decided them.

'I want to avenge my mother and the others like her who have fallen to the firesticks of poachers.'

Even Orang Tua did not argue. He noted that the young tiger speaking with such passion had the tufty fur around his face of a beast that had not reached adulthood. Man was taking a terrible toll on the creatures of the rainforests if a big cat, who was really no more than a kitten, was representing his species at a Council of Beasts.

Whether they were fighting for time to rescue the Seeds or just lashing out in anger at the humans that could kill a creature as magnificent as a tiger for a trophy hide and some useless medicines, Orang Tua no longer felt like resisting. They would fight on.

The plan of attack, outlined by the rhino, was simple. They would split up into groups of twenty animals. Pythons and an eagle to scout ahead, orang utans to sabotage the generators, cobras to kill the ringleaders, a main attack by the tigers and elephants and then a quick, silent retreat into the jungle. Extra care would be taken not to set anything on fire and light up the camp. The pitch blackness of the night was the chief advantage the animals had over the humans. They needed to preserve it at all costs. And this time they would target every major camp in Borneo. It was to be an all out assault.

'Are there any questions?' asked the rhino curtly.

There were head shakes all around. The beasts understood what they had to do.

The rhino looked up. The pale crescent moon glowed in the night sky.

The rhino said, 'It will take a while for the teams attacking the camps further away to get into position. We will attack on the first night that heavy clouds hide the face of the waxing moon. Wait for word.'

There was no argument from the beasts. The velvet darkness of the jungle when the moon had hidden her face was the perfect time for an attack.

• • •

The plan to retrieve the oil from Alaska's North Shore was simple. Lay down the infrastructure – pipelines and roads – for transporting the oil from the well sites. At the same time, prepare for drilling – onshore and offshore oil rigs – to be ready to pump the minute the exit route was ready. But Valentine had one more trick up his sleeve.

He said to his aides, including Spencer's father, 'Consider a location for a refinery.'

'A refinery?' asked one of the men. 'Why?'

'This planet is getting darned hot. You know and I know that Arctic winter ice will disappear completely over the summer months.'

'But that's tens of years away,' protested an aide.

'Don't you worry about it! At the rate I'm cutting down rainforests, Arctic sea ice is gonna be gone a long time before that.'

An oilman said, his eyes shining with excitement, 'A refinery on the North Shore would allow us to ship processed oil over the open seas across the North Pole towards markets all over the Northern Hemisphere!'

'Exactly,' said Valentine. 'The cost savings will make any oil we can squeeze out of this Alaskan rock and ice very cost effective. But remember,' he looked warningly at his team, 'This is top secret for now. I don't want to give the green lobby another stick to beat me with – not yet.'

• • •

The owl was very impatient, urging Honesty to get going to Alaska. But there were tickets to buy, warm clothes to borrow, an itinerary to plan. It hadn't been possible to just drop everything and climb on a plane. They planned to go from London to New York, New York to Anchorage in Alaska and from Anchorage to Fairbanks. From Fairbanks, they would fly to an airstrip outside an Inuit village near the north Alaska coast and then make the short, overland trek to the foot of the Arrigetch peaks.

Jane was a bit taken aback that Honesty was not content to just admire the aurora borealis from Fairbanks and wanted to trek up and down mountains as well.

But Honesty was adamant. 'We might see a grizzly or a polar bear, Mum!' She continued, 'Or a narwhal …'

'What's that?'

'A sea unicorn.'

Mum looked mystified.

Finally, after a month of preparation, they were dragging their bags across bumpy pavements at Heathrow and being glared at by policemen with machine guns. They were forced to repack all their bags at the gate and cram their hand luggage into a single bag. Their bottles of water were confiscated. This caused an argument between Jane and the airport staff.

'Any liquids in your hand luggage, madam?' a young woman asked politely.

'Just some water for the plane.'

'I need to take that.'

'What do you mean?'

'No liquids allowed. You can buy some more once you're through the departure gates.'

'But I don't want to buy water.'

'Alright, but you're not allowed to take this water on board.'

The people in the queue behind Jane were getting annoyed and the men with guns moved closer.

'Mum,' Honesty said urgently, 'Let's just leave the water.'

'But I'm not going to buy a bottle of water! You know how I feel about bottled water …'

There was a muttering in the crowd.

The security lady had looked relieved though. 'Ma'am, you can just empty the water, keep your container and fill it up again at the water cooler.'

Jane's face brightened. She tipped the water out to ironic cheers from the queue and marched through the security check.

Honesty hurried after her. Her knees felt trembly and weak with relief. They were on their way.

• • •

Spencer was at Fairbanks airport waiting for the helicopter that would take him out to the ice plains. He was eavesdropping on a conversation among a group of big men. He had not meant to listen. He was sitting quietly – sleepy from their early start that morning but excited that they were ready to set out for the ice again. Dad had been reluctant to take him. But Spencer was so upset at the thought of being left behind that in the end he had relented, warning the boy that there was serious work to be done and he must not get in the way. Spencer barely heard him. He was so thrilled to be going back north of the Arctic Circle.

But listening to the men, he knew what Dad had been talking about when he mentioned 'serious work'. These big men with ruddy cheeks and red noses from years of exposure to the cold were discussing prospecting for oil. They were from Point Barrow, where the oil rigs and refineries were. And they were as excited as Spencer to be heading out onto the ice, but for quite different reasons.

In a laconic drawl, one of them said, 'It's a big one.'

'How big?' one of the others asked, eyes gleaming at the thought of the black gold waiting to be recovered from under the icy ground.

'No one is saying, for sure,' the first man continued. 'But the scientists think the seams run from the coastal plains right up to the foothills of the Brookes Range.'

'That's a lot of oil!' exclaimed another smaller, wiry man with only one ear; the other had been lost to frostbite. He continued, 'It's not going to be easy to suck out – I hear the pockets are small and deep.'

They all nodded. This was a job they understood. Recovering oil from difficult terrain was their expertise.

'That new scientist the boss hired – it seems he knows

where the oil is …'

'Is the equipment on its way?' another asked.

'There ain't a piece of machinery that might help us squeeze oil out of the land which is not being dragged, carried, shipped, trucked and carted out there onto the tundra,' laughed the first one.

Spencer leapt to his feet and grabbed the edge of the man's coat, tugging it to get his attention.

The man looked down at the spiky-haired, angry boy in surprise. 'Hey there, young fellow. What's up?'

'You're taking oil stuff to the ice? But the polar bears will be coming in to den soon!'

The men looked puzzled.

Spencer said urgently, 'The polar bears … they come off the ice to den on the coast.'

One of the men laughed. 'Well, looks like they're gonna have to find a new address this year.'

Spencer was almost shouting, 'It's an Arctic refuge … a wildlife refuge. You're not allowed to drill there!'

The wiry man chuckled, 'Where've you been, boy? Rules have changed. We need that oil now. A darn sight more than we need some overgrown teddy bears.'

'What's going on here?'

Spencer whirled around in relief. 'Dad, these men say they're drilling for oil at the refuge – but it's not allowed, right? Tell them it's not allowed!'

His Dad flushed. 'I'm afraid they've changed the rules, son.'

The oilman who had first spoken was staring intently at Spencer's Dad. Now he said, 'Hang on a minute! Aren't you Dr. Richard Jones?'

Spencer's Dad nodded reluctantly. All the men were wreathed in smiles, shaking his hand and slapping him on the back.

'What's going on, Dad? How do these people know you?'

'How do we know your Dad? Young man, this here's the man that found us all that oil. Without him, the black gold might have stayed underground for another thousand years!'

Spencer turned and ran out of the airport.

-twenty five-

It really was embarrassing, thought Honesty. The owl had promised to send word of her arrival through the higher birds in case she needed any help in Alaska. And she had been as good as her word. The higher Alaskan birds certainly knew she was coming. They were treating her like a celebrity.

It started at Anchorage airport where three bald eagles sat on the telephone wires and shrieked her name loudly and excitedly. Bald eagles were not as rare as they had once been. But very few people in Anchorage had ever seen a flock. Three noisy, endangered birds on a wire, the beautiful white plumage on their heads and tails shining in the sun, certainly caused a stir. Fortunately, thought Honesty, no one except her could understand what they were saying.

'Welcome to Alaska,' they squawked.

'You will save the Borneo beasts! We know you will.'

'Good luck on your quest for the Seeds.'

'Call us if you need anything!'

Honestly, thought Honesty, they sounded as daft as the

chickens she'd left behind.

The short flight to Fairbanks was even worse. The birds flew alongside the small plane like a fighter escort. If any got tired or were left behind, others took their place. The passengers on board, old Alaska hands most of them, could not believe what they were seeing. They pointed and laughed and exclaimed in amazement to see so many eagles, hawks and kites. Honesty resolutely read a magazine. She was terrified one of the silly creatures would crash into the plane if she took any notice of them.

When they landed, Honesty grabbed her small bag and hurried into the terminal. She did not want to draw attention to herself. Being chased by a posse of excited birds was no way to avoid notice. Jane went to find out where their hotel was and Honesty ducked into the gift shop. There were books and postcards of Alaska in the window. She wanted to have another look for the 'green mountain'. Honesty hurriedly turned the pages of a few glossy guidebooks. There was nothing remotely green in the way of mountains. She gave up and wandered over to the revolving postcard display. There were hundreds of pictures of the northern lights and she stared at them awestruck. It was no wonder the Collective Memory of these waves of intense colour had not faded over the generations.

Honesty was distracted by the sound of muffled, angry sobbing. She looked around. On a bench, just outside the shop, a boy of about her age was sitting with his face in his hands.

Honesty asked timidly, 'I say, are you alright?'

There was no answer. She said again, 'Are you ok? Are you lost or something? I'm sure my Mum could help.'

The boy looked up at her and wiped his eyes with his knuckles. He said, 'I'm fine, thanks.'

Honesty said doubtfully, 'You don't look fine.'

She wondered if he had run away. He did not seem to be with anyone. She remembered her own experience in London and a shadow crossed her face.

She asked politely, 'You haven't run away from home, have you? It's just that I did that once. It's a terrible idea.'

The boy shook his head and she noticed his spiky black hair for the first time. 'I haven't run away.' He turned the thought around in his head. 'But maybe I should,' he continued bitterly.

'Please don't,' said Honesty earnestly.

'How would you feel if you'd just discovered that your Dad, your own Dad, was the one who found the oil and all these people are going to drill in the wildlife refuge and there isn't going to be anywhere for the polar bears?'

Honesty had done a lot of reading on Alaska recently so she understood the convoluted protest.

'That is bad luck,' Honesty said sympathetically. 'Did he really discover the oil?'

'I think they knew it was there all along. But he's found out exactly where it is and how to get it out too.'

Honesty nodded. She said, 'I'm Honesty, by the way.'

The boy did not appear to notice her peculiar name. They shook hands with slightly embarrassed formality.

'I'm Spencer,' he said.

Honesty's mother appeared in the distance and beckoned to her.

'That's my Mum,' said Honesty. 'I have to go.' She continued anxiously, 'But you won't run away, will you?'

Spencer shook his head. 'No. I'll have to think of something though.'

Honesty gave him a quick smile of sympathy and ran to her mother.

All trips out of Fairbanks airport were postponed that day. Apparently, the weather across Alaska was stormy. Honesty was disappointed but prepared to be reasonable about the twenty-four hour delay. Every moment of this quest was important. On the other hand, it was extraordinary that she was in Alaska. She would have pinched herself to make sure it was not a dream except that her hands were in thick (borrowed) gloves and it was too much bother to take them off.

Jane insisted on walking up and down the streets and alleys of the small town to look for lunch. She was convinced that there would be an organic vegetarian restaurant. If there was one, it had not been possible to find it. At last, Jane agreed on a diner and they ate chips and drank chocolate milkshakes while Jane muttered in an undertone about salt, monosodium glutamate and the plight of cocoa farmers in the Third World.

At least, thought Honesty, she had managed to shake the birds. The higher birds had escorted them through the first two streets until Honesty had an idea. She knelt down to tie her shoe laces, letting her mother wander ahead.

'You've got to stop following me around,' she whispered urgently to the bald eagle who seemed to be the leader.

'We have been tasked with keeping you safe,' the bird said firmly.

'There's no danger here. But people might notice that you lot are acting eccentric,' Honesty protested.

'I don't know what you mean,' squawked the bird huffily, turning its head to stare at Honesty with one full, golden eye.

Honesty gazed around frantically and then had a brainwave.

'There is something you can do,' she said. 'A sort of mini-quest!'

The birds screeched excitedly, puffed up their chest feathers and preened themselves.

'What is it? What is it?'

'A green mountain.'

Blank looks greeted her request.

'A green mountain … it's the last clue. I need to know where it is to find the Seeds.'

'What do you want us to do?'

'Find it!'

• • •

Spencer refused to speak to his Dad. But he did rejoin

the expedition. He was determined to save his polar bear friends. But he could not do that unless he was out on the ice too. That meant going with his Dad to the coastal plains. He had to go with him – but he sure didn't have to talk to him. But they were stuck in Fairbanks too. No one was going to risk the storm front between Fairbanks and the Arctic Sea in a helicopter.

The next day, as they arrived at the terminal once more to try to get to the North Shore, a private jet screamed into the airport. Spencer watched it land in awe – it was so sleek and small and powerful. He noticed the Texic logo, an oil spout against a green background, on the tail.

As he sat impatiently in a plastic chair at the airport, he heard a commotion at immigration. Spencer saw men with microphones and cameras rush forward. His heart sank. It sat at the bottom of his stomach like too much rich chocolate cake.

Elliot Valentine stepped through the checkpoint wearing a full-length mink fur coat. A grey wolf walked sedately by his side. As the press converged on him, Valentine pushed up his large designer sunglasses until they were perched on his forehead like a spare pair of eyes. He beamed at the press. 'Gentlemen, of course I will make a statement. But no questions. There is work to be done.'

He took a few steps forward and was surrounded by a bank of microphones. 'I am here to personally supervise the commencement of drilling operations. I want to be on the spot to make sure that we extract the maximum oil with the minimum damage to the wildlife refuge. Thank you for your kind attention.'

He was assaulted with a barrage of questions.

'Mr. Valentine, how can you be sure that there will be no damage to the environment?'

'Mr. Valentine, what do you say to scientists who claim there isn't enough oil there to be worth the effort?'

'Mr. Valentine, what about global warming?'

'Mr. Valentine, how about the polar bears?'

The fat man put up a small, pudgy, four-fingered hand and the voices fell silent. 'I said no questions! But I would like to introduce you to someone without whom this whole effort would have been in vain.'

The ringed hand gestured imperiously. Spencer saw his Dad standing quietly behind the group of reporters. The crowd parted and Spencer's Dad joined his boss at the front.

'This is the man, Richard Jones, whom we have to thank.'

There was a round of polite applause.

It was interrupted by a high clear voice, 'You should be ashamed of yourself! Destroying one of the last great wildlife reserves for a few barrels of oil. How much did he pay you? Thirty pieces of silver? I hope you think it's worth it.'

And the next thing that happened was that an egg, an ordinary brown breakfast egg, came sailing through the air and hit Elliot Valentine square on the head. It was hard-boiled.

Spencer saw that the egg had been thrown by a beautiful, middle-aged woman. She was surrounded by a group of people including the girl he had met the previous day, the one called Honesty. He recognised the yelling woman – she was Honesty's mother. Soon, all the protesters were shouting and screaming. A few made their way towards Valentine, determined expressions on their faces. Security guards and police hurried to intervene. Valentine's bodyguards bundled him towards the waiting helicopter. They dragged Spencer's Dad with them. He was anxiously scanning the crowd for Spencer. When he spotted him, he yelled something to one of the guards. Spencer was picked off the ground by a burly man dressed in black, slung over the man's shoulder like a sack of potatoes and hurried towards his father. In a moment, all three were in the chopper. The wolf leapt in after them.

The rotor blades were spinning furiously and the helicopter lifted off the ground. The rush of wind stopped the group of men that had been charging the aircraft. They shook their fists and shouted after them. Spencer's last view of the now toy-sized people was of them being overrun by airport security.

'Damned hippies!' muttered Valentine angrily, patting the spot on his forehead that had been hit by the egg with a large handkerchief. 'I hope they lock them up and throw away the key.'

Spencer did not say anything. Inside he was exultant. Others were trying to stop the drilling too. He was not alone. He just hoped that the girl's mother would not get into too much trouble.

• • •

Honesty's mother and the rest of the protesters were arrested by the converging security. A massive policeman, beer belly straining to escape his shirt, escorted them towards the waiting police vans. Honesty was separated from her mother. As she tried to fight through the crowds, her mother waved her away with an imperious gesture.

'Find a payphone,' she yelled. 'Call your father! Tell him what's happened.' Her last words were muffled as the van doors slammed shut.

Tell her Dad what had happened. Honesty sat down on a large rock outside the airport. What in the world was she to tell him? That they had finished their dinner of chips and milkshakes, sauntered over to the motel they had booked for the night, only to find themselves at the headquarters of various anti-drilling activists. The protesters had come in all shapes and sizes. Some, Honesty had noticed, were smelly and angry. But there were also scientists, politicians, mothers with bundled-up babies and spotty teenagers with 'save the bear' t-shirts.

And her own Mum, quiet, placid, unruffled Mum, had been inspired. She had listened and watched and signed petitions to various governments and the United Nations. Later that morning, when their departure had coincided with that of the protesters, Honesty's Mum had stayed with the group at the airport and listened to Valentine's smug remarks until her blood was up. She had tried to shout the oilmen down. When that didn't work, she lobbed the egg that she had saved for a snack. And hit Valentine. As she said, golden hair askew and chest heaving, to the policeman as they were led to waiting police vans – it was the best use to which she could have put a non-free range egg.

Honesty supposed there was a point beyond which Mum could not be pushed. But this was a fine time for them to have discovered it. She really was stuck. She stood up and stretched. The hard rock was terribly uncomfortable. She had better find a payphone and try and explain their plight to Dad.

A security guard sauntered over. He was Inuit, Honesty could see that at a glance. He asked, 'Are you alright?'

She saw that he was genuinely concerned.

'Well, they've got my Mum,' she said, a lot more bravely than she felt.

'I thought you were with them. A brave lot – trying to save the wildlife refuge. I grew up around there. I can't believe that they're planning on digging it up for oil. I'm afraid your Mum might be doing some time.'

'For throwing an egg?'

'Well, they'll be trying to set an example with this lot. To discourage other anarchists.'

'Anarchists!'

'Well, she did throw an egg,' pointed out the security guard.

'How long will she get?'

'Three months …'

Honesty's mind was working furiously. What in the world was she to do? She could call her Dad. But how was she going to get the Seeds?

The guard said, awkwardly twisting his hat in his hands, 'Look, I'm really sorry about this. What are you going to do? Can I help in any way?'

Honesty did not answer. She looked around, seeking a solution to her quandary and her eyes lit on the large, green rock she'd been sitting on earlier.

'What's that?' she asked absently.

'The rock?'

'Yes.'

'It's a piece of Jade Mountain.'

'I beg your pardon?'

'You know, Jade Mountain. That's why Alaska's state gemstone is jade.'

He had her attention.

He continued, 'You must have heard of it. It's a big green mountain … made of solid jade.'

She asked quietly, barely daring to hope, 'Where is it?'

'The five fingers of the Arrigetch peaks? They're known as the gates to the Arctic sometimes?'

She nodded to indicate she had heard of them.

'Well, the index finger is Jade Mountain.'

-twenty six-

Spencer leapt out of the helicopter the minute it landed and headed towards the camp ahead of his father. He soon spotted Ataneq. The Inuit was delighted to see him and slapped him on the back and then hugged him tight.

Spencer asked, 'Do you know what they're doing?'

The Inuit hunter's eyes narrowed in his weather-beaten face.

'What shall we do?' Spencer asked urgently.

Ataneq looked out over the unspoilt horizon. Spencer followed his gaze. He guessed that the Inuit was imagining it bristling with oil rigs and pipelines.

He said, 'What can we do? You're a child and I am an Inuit hunter. How can we do anything?'

Spencer said, 'I don't know. But I'm going to try.'

He trudged off towards the sea. The cold wind came whipping in and he pulled his jacket tighter around himself. It was early winter now and the temperatures had plunged. He was wearing multiple layers, a traditional parka with a hood, mittens and thick hardy, warm boots.

The sun was at its zenith, but was so low in the sky it cast only a pale unconvincing light over the icy terrain.

His next words were seized by the wind and flung at his friend, 'But first I have to find the polar bears.'

• • •

Honesty walked slowly towards the jailhouse wondering what to do. She had found her green mountain. All the clues were in place. She knew where the Seeds were. If she called her Dad, he would tell her to stay put and fly out to join them as soon as he could. He would spend every moment trying to get her mother out of jail. Then they would go back to England, money and energy exhausted. The Seeds would be lost as the search for oil began. She would have failed Kai.

She desperately wanted to see Mum. But Honesty was afraid that if the police realised that she was on her own, they might pass her to social services or worse, arrest her too. Honesty sat down on a sidewalk bench and wondered what to do.

A stern voice said, 'That was your mother, wasn't it?'

Honesty looked up and saw a bony woman with crinkly iron grey hair. She recognised her as one of the scarier protesters from the motel.

'What's the matter? Cat got your tongue?'

Honesty roused herself to say, 'I beg your pardon?'

'The egg – that was your mother, wasn't it?'

'Yes, ma'am.'

Honesty looked around nervously in case the woman in her assorted, ill-fitting sweaters turned out to be a lunatic.

The woman smiled broadly and immediately looked less like a witch and more like the kind but firm headmistress of a girls' boarding school. 'A fine shot. You should be proud!'

'I am,' said Honesty firmly. But then her face fell.

'What's the matter?'

'Nothing … I just really need to get to the ice.'

'Your Mum will be out in a few days, I'm sure.'

'I hope so …'

'What about your Dad?'

'He's in England.'

A group of green activists came up to them, hailing the old lady politely. Most of them had been at the motel the previous evening. When they saw Honesty, there was much back-slapping and high-fiving.

A man with beautiful long blonde hair tied into a ponytail said, 'Your Mum, she's a hero – she struck the first blow!'

Honesty looked glum.

'Hey kid! What's up?'

'We might end up going back to England without ever getting out to the wildlife reserve.'

There were murmurs of easy sympathy.

Honesty looked at them and had a brainwave. She said, 'You could help me!'

'Sure kid, anything,' said the man with the ponytail.

'You could let me come with you to the ice.'

There was a silence while they thought about it. A young, suburban woman carrying a baby wrapped like a papoose, said, 'Why not? You could come with us, I guess. We'll be back in a few days anyway. Your Mum would have been released by then.'

Honesty looked up, her face radiant, 'May I, really?'

'Of course,' said the old woman. 'It's the least we can do for your mother. You need to go and ask her though.'

Honesty nodded enthusiastically, her red curls bouncing up and down. 'I'll do that right now.'

'Alright. Then meet us back at the motel. We leave first thing in the morning.'

Honesty took off at a quick trot. She turned a corner and dived into an alley. There was no way Mum would let her wander off to a protest gathering with a bunch of hippies. Honesty was in no position to live up to her name. She would have to lie.

She wondered a bit at these wildlife activists who were prepared to take the word of an eleven year old girl that her imprisoned mother had no objection to her traipsing across the Arctic in their company. Then she realised these people were in the fight of their lives. To them, Jane was the first casualty – and the first martyr – of the battle. It seemed natural that she would want her daughter to carry the torch for the family.

Honesty wrote a note to Mum, assuring her that she

234

was fine and just waiting for Dad at the motel. She asked the friendly security guard to deliver it. Next she rang Dad when she knew he would be fast asleep and left a brief message explaining what had happened to Mum. She suggested that she would sit tight until he rode in to the rescue. And then, her conscience heavy, but her heart light, she went back and told the group that Mum would be delighted if they took her with them.

And so a day late and minus her mother, Honesty was packed into a small aeroplane and flown to the North Shore of Alaska. As the coast narrowed, she saw the five beckoning fingers of the Arrigetch mountains. The small plane rose a little higher and flew through the gap between the two tallest peaks, the middle finger and the index finger of the beckoning hand. Honesty gazed out of the window at Jade Mountain. It did not look any different from the others, the surface was the same weathered rock – vegetation was thickest, closest to ground level. But Honesty had no doubt it was the right place. The Jade Mountain just had to be the 'green mountain' of animal legend.

As the plane came in low in a wide sweep, Honesty could see that there were already piles of heavy machinery on the ice-covered tundra. There were deep ruts criss-crossing the coastal plains as well. One of the others told her it was the tyre tracks of four wheel drive vehicles dashing about their oily business.

There was a small camp with collapsible tents, a generator and a small helicopter parked on the ice. A Kiwi protester from Greenpeace, who had cut his teeth boarding whaling boats, pointed at the camp and said in his southern hemisphere drawl, 'That's the enemy HQ, boys and girls!'

Honesty could see a young boy and an adult walking away from the camp. She wondered if it was the scientist's son, Spencer, who was so upset at his father's involvement in the planned destruction. There was no way to find out. The pair disappeared over the horizon as the plane came in to land on a small airstrip outside the biggest Inuit village in the Arctic refuge.

• • •

It *was* Spencer, out for the second day in a row looking for his polar bear friends. So far there was no sign of them. He was very worried. He could see that Ataneq had grave doubts about whether the polar bears were alive. They had never had this much trouble finding them before. Despite the vastness of the icy plain, the bears had always picked up the scent of the man bear and his Inuit friend and come out to meet them. But now Spencer sucked the icy air into his lungs and hollered and yelled and called and his words were whipped across the ice and scattered in every direction but no polar bears responded.

When he had almost given up hope, the bears appeared, bounding over a ridge, pounding down the sides, all three of them, thin but safe – and happy to see their man bear friend. Spencer hugged them and they nuzzled him and for a short time it did seem that things were going to be alright.

But as they sat down together mother bear said, 'Things have changed since you went away, man bear. The humans are everywhere. Do you know what's going on?'

Spencer hung his head and said, 'They are looking for oil.'

'Oil? The slimy black liquid that oozes out of the ground and mats our fur so that we freeze to death?'

'Yes.'

'But why?'

'Humans use it to power cars and aeroplanes.'

'But why have they come here? They never did before.'

Spencer could have told them about what his Dad had done. Instead he said, 'They think they know where the oil is and how to get it out cheaply.'

The more boisterous of the young ones interrupted them, 'But where is this oil?'

Spencer looked around him at the rolling tundra. 'Everywhere, I'm afraid. It's everywhere.'

• • •

The group Honesty was with soon numbered about fifty. Men and women, self-important or earnest, fun-loving or frightened, they were all there to stop the drilling. Honesty mingled but did not say much. She had only one goal – to get to Jade Mountain as soon as she could.

She asked the Inuit villagers the best way and they laughed – their strong, white teeth gleaming in their weather-beaten faces. They were amused at the child's fascination with jade. They scratched diagrams in the snow to show her the way to Jade Mountain. It was towards one end of the mountain range that formed the southern boundary to the wildlife refuge. Further east, the range ran close to the sea. Jade Mountain was right against the coast. During winter, the sea ice reached up to the foothills.

And, they added, twinkling at her, sometimes big chunks of jade would break off the mountain in a storm and could be picked up with bare hands. 'Although a scrawny young thing like you might not be strong enough to lift a nice piece of jade,' a plump woman with two thick plaits of black hair and a beautifully embroidered jacket, said to general laughter.

'What's the best way to get there?' asked Honesty.

'Well now, a team of huskies would do,' said one of the men. 'You could hire a guide and make a trip if the weather was right. Not something you can do on your own, of course. Riding a team of huskies takes years of training.'

Honesty thought hard. The last thing she wanted was a guide while she tried to find the Seeds.

That evening she snuck out of her motel room and slipped out into the crisp night. There was complete silence in the small village and Honesty felt very small and cold. She hurried down the main strip, not a road so much as packed snow with snowmobile tracks. She knew exactly where she was going. She had made sure to find out earlier that day.

It did not take her long to find the barn where the huskies were kept indoors at night for warmth. The barn was not locked and she slid the bolt, heaving a sigh of relief that it was well-oiled. The huskies had been asleep, curled up in snug corners for warmth. But they were awake now, ears pricking up and pale eyes with narrow pupils gazing at her in the half-light cast by an oil lamp.

She whispered, 'My name is Honesty. I'm on an important quest. I need your help.'

None of the dogs responded. They continued to look at her with mystified expressions. Honesty felt a wave of disappointment. She knew from experience that domesticated animals were daft, but she had hoped that these dogs, living so close to nature at the very top of the world, might retain enough natural ability to help.

She spoke again, an urgent whisper through cracked and cold lips, 'Do you understand me? I am trying to save the animals of Borneo. Can anyone help me?'

From the depths of the barn a large, pepper and salt husky limped towards her. It sniffed the hand she held out and then sat down on its haunches and looked at her, 'I understand you,' he said. 'What do you want?'

Honesty sank to her knees on the hay until she was looking at the old beast eye to eye. She said, 'The Higher Beasts are looking for Seeds from the beginning of time. I know where they are, I need help to get them.'

'What do you need?'

'A team of huskies to take me to Jade Mountain tomorrow night.'

'Very well. I will arrange it. I cannot pull a sled anymore,' he lifted his front paw to show Honesty a foot that was missing half the pad, 'but I will come along to instruct the dogs.'

'Thank you,' said Honesty.

The next day she planned her trip carefully. She stockpiled as many sandwiches as she could and two big bottles of water. She packed matches in an oilskin and stored all the warm clothes she was not wearing in her backpack. She would need every bit of clothing not to freeze to death as the temperatures plunged at night.

The protesters were planning to march on Valentine's camp the following day. Honesty was relieved. In the excitement, no one, not even the young couple who had appointed themselves her unofficial guardians, would notice that she had slipped away in the night. The team of huskies would be missed, of course. But there was no reason anyone would suspect her of having anything to do with it.

Almost everyone at the camp was jumpy. Otherwise, Honesty's restlessness would have been noticed. She could not sit still. She wandered around the village, fought the temptation to check on the dogs, declined the offer of a taste of whale blubber, worried about her Mum and wondered what Dad was doing. Trying to get a flight, no doubt.

She was wrong. Her Dad was on a plane to New York

even as she imagined him quarrelling with travel agents. The incident with Jane and the egg was caught on film. Once again, her father was dragged out by the neighbours to watch the news on television. But this time it was not his daughter hogging the limelight, but his wife. The impassioned speech and the accuracy of her throw had immediately turned the record of events into the most downloaded clip on YouTube. It wasn't often that a beautiful woman accurately threw an egg at an oil tycoon. The evening news had followed up with the story. No mention was made of a daughter. Honesty's father caught the first available flight. He was long gone by the time Honesty left her message on the answer phone.

• • •

Spencer tried to persuade the bears to hold a meeting. They were reluctant. The polar bear is by nature a loner, trekking across the ice in a silent, age-old quest for food. But at last they agreed to talk. The gathering was planned for that evening. Spencer would have to sneak out and head for the rendezvous. He was looking forward to it. He needed to do something to fix the damage Dad was planning for the perfect landscape around him.

• • •

That night, Honesty saw the northern lights for the

first time. Shades of purple and pink filled the sky as she slipped out of the motel for the second night running. The waves glistened and shimmered and faded and intensified and turned the inky black night into the most beautiful palette Honesty had ever seen. She stood stock still, barely noticing the cold grabbing at her with icy fingers. It must be a good omen, she decided hopefully. The first clue to the Seeds – the waves of light – was lighting up the night sky.

The dogs were awake and milling around. The husky, who told her his name was Qannik, was limping back and forth, giving the dogs instructions in quiet yelps. When Honesty snuck into the barn, he buried his cold nose in the palm of her hand as a welcoming gesture. Then it was down to business. He barked advice on how to hitch up the sled to the dogs. It was hard work. Honesty was not sure she was strong enough to buckle the harnesses and tighten the ropes. Qannik kept the dogs in order and they stood patiently while she worked away with numb, cold fingers. At last it was done. She loaded up her food and drink. Qannik showed her where the dog food, frozen reindeer meat, was kept and she loaded some of that too.

Qannik himself led the dogs out. They followed his quietly whined instructions to the letter. Honesty climbed onto the sled and the huskies pulled her away. The harnesses jingled and rattled. She was terrified someone would wake up and spot them but they made a clean escape. Once they were beyond the village limits, Qannik barked a command and the dogs broke into a quick, even trot. He ran with them, maintaining the same pace, occasionally nipping back and forth, like a good sheepdog, ensuring that all the dogs were keeping up. Honesty just had to hang on and hope as they turned their noses towards Jade Mountain.

-twenty seven-

The moon was full and yet invisible. Huge black clouds hid it from all eyes. It was late evening. The rhino stood silently, contemplating the twilight. The silhouette of trees was barely visible against the dark indigo sky. It would be very dark tonight. Darker even than when the moon had waned to nothing because the thick clouds were obscuring even the distant glimmer of stars. They could launch the second wave of attacks.

The rhino had a moment of concern. Even under the canopy, the silvery light of the full moon would reveal far too much to the humans. He looked again at the storm clouds. Would they dissipate suddenly and expose the beasts? He doubted it. These had the solidity and permanence of an early monsoon storm. The rhino did not want to wait. Not when he had already waited so long. Not when his revenge against Man depended on a bunch of animals overcoming their natural instinct to turn on each other and fight the humans instead. He said to Burung, the brahminy kite, 'Tell the others. It is tonight.'

• • •

Spencer woke up and got dressed just after midnight. He dragged on his woollen parka and slipped on his mittens. Like Honesty, he stopped to admire the intensity of the northern lights and their terrifying other-worldly beauty. He had no huskies to summon so he set a brisk walking pace. The meeting place was at least an hour away. There was no time to waste.

No one saw Spencer disappear into the night. No person, that is. Tarzan the wolf saw him go. The big, grey beast got to his feet, stretched quickly and opened his jaws in a tongue-curling, fang-baring yawn. Then he slunk out of the camp, his bushy tail tucked in behind him and set off in quiet pursuit of the boy.

• • •

The northern lights were blue (every shade from indigo to azure) and purple (claret to lavender) now and, away from the lights of the village, even more intense. The aurora was reflected on the snow-covered ground. To Honesty, it was as if she was mushing through a new landscape, not in or of the world at all. A mysterious place where heaven and earth were mirror images and it did not matter whether she was gliding through air or on land. She knew she was being fanciful and the rattling of the harnesses and the odd bark or whine of a dog were reassuringly ordinary in this strange world.

• • •

Spencer, the man bear, found the rest of his tribe. He had never seen so many polar bears in one place before and he suspected no one else had either. There were old bears with patchy fur and scarred faces from a lifetime of battling for territory and for food. There were worried mothers with their cubs, determined to try and save their babies from this new threat. And there were young males standing tall on their hind legs, aggressive, ready for a fight and reluctant to listen to the warnings of the elders.

Spencer was very quiet. He listened to the bears discussing their options and worried for their future. But he was just a cub and knew that it was not his place to speak at this gathering.

Unknown to him and carefully downwind of the bears, a grey wolf watched proceedings with interest.

• • •

Honesty did not know it because the old husky was too proud to mention it – but Qannik had completely lost his sense of smell in the same incident that had cost him half his foot. It was the result of a severe case of frostbite. Once when Qannik was lead dog, he and his master were caught unawares by a blizzard. None of the other team dogs had made it through the storm. Qannik and his master had huddled together and been found by a search and rescue team after the storm had passed. Both had survived. But his master had lost two fingers and Qannik half a paw and his sense of smell.

His lost sense of smell mattered because Qannik was in charge. It mattered because the dogs were mushing forward under his guidance. It mattered because there was a meeting of polar bears going on over the next crest.

None of the polar bears noticed the approaching team of huskies. They might have got a whiff of dog in the air if they were paying attention but they were too busy arguing over the best thing to do to combat the advance of Man into the North. The polar bears' fur glowed many colours under the northern lights.

The huskies came bounding over the hill in perfect unison.

Chaos reigned.

The dogs panicked. Howling and barking they pulled and yanked at their restraints, determined to escape. The harnesses, tied more loosely than normal by Honesty's cold fingers, gave way. The huskies scattered. Miraculously, the sled stayed upright. Qannik raced after it as it shot down the hill. It gathered pace. Honesty clung on. For a few seconds, it seemed that she might just race through the ranks of stunned polar bears and burst through the other side. Then the sled hit a rock. It catapulted into the air. Honesty was flung off like a rag doll and hit the ground hard – right in the middle of the bears.

The bears' first instinct, when the dogs had come bursting

over the crest, was to run. The largest predator on the ice did not fear dogs. But in their experience, dogs meant men and men meant guns. But then it became obvious that the dogs were out of control. As the huskies broke free and dashed off into the night, the bears saw the sled, with just one small human on it, careering down the hill. They gaped as it flew through the air and dislodged the human. They watched her crash to the ground at their feet. The big dog, who had not tried to escape, raced up to the human and stood guard over her, teeth bared and hackles raised.

The bears were angry and worried. But they were indecisive as well. An individual bear would have killed the dog immediately. As a group they were not sure what to do. They growled and reared and waited for one of the others to take the lead.

Honesty sat up and tried to wipe away the snow and ice that caked her eyes and nostrils. She was badly shaken and a big bruise was developing on her forehead. She knew that she was sitting on the ground surrounded by polar bears. But the enormity of the moment was too much for her. All she knew was that her team of dogs was gone and with it her chance of getting the Seeds.

It took Spencer a few moments to recognise Honesty. He was so taken aback by her dramatic entrance – and fearful for the safety of the bears – that he had not realised that the intruder was just a child. Now as she sat up and he recognised her, he rushed forward, struggling past the bears until he was on his knees next to her.

He said, 'Honesty?'

She stared at him in astonishment.

Spencer said again, 'Honesty? Are you alright?'

She frowned and put a hand to the bruise on her forehead. 'Just winded, I think.'

'You know this child?' one of the older bears asked gravely.

'We've met,' said Spencer.

'At the airport,' added Honesty.

The two children looked at each other.

It was Honesty who spoke first. 'You understand them? The bears, I mean?' she asked timidly.

Spencer nodded. 'You do too?'

It was Honesty's turn to nod.

-twenty eight-

'But what are you doing here?' asked Honesty, getting to her feet shakily and making the question general enough to encompass the polar bears.

'Trying to decide what to do about the plans to drill for oil in the Arctic refuge,' answered Spencer. The polar bears growled their assent.

'But how about you? Why are you out here on the ice on your own? You're just a cub!' It was the mother bear who had befriended Spencer asking.

Honesty wrinkled her nose. 'I'm not sure you'd believe me if I told you.'

'Go on,' urged Spencer. 'Tell us! Do you have a plan? It was your Mum that threw the egg at Valentine, wasn't it?'

'Is that his name? Yes, that was my Mum. She's in prison for three months.'

Spencer was horrified, 'I'm terribly sorry,' he said, very conscious of his Dad's part in the unfolding disaster.

The polar bears were growing restless, not really understanding the girl's story.

Spencer explained, 'This girl's mother attacked the chief of the oil company. But she's been put in a cage for three moons as punishment!'

There were angry growls from the polar bears when they heard this. One of the younger ones nuzzled Honesty in gentle sympathy. She hugged the beast and winked at Spencer, 'Great translation!'

He grinned back, 'I've had a bit of practice. But please, what are you doing here?'

Honesty told them. She sat down cross-legged on the ground and tried to ignore the cold seeping into her bones. The old husky lay down next to her and she was glad of his warm, furry body. The polar bears sat or stood or lay down in a semi-circle around her, listening to every word. Spencer waited a few feet away, with his arm around one of the young bears and focussed intently on Honesty as her amazing tale unfolded.

Honesty left nothing out. She told them of the orang utans of Borneo and the deforestation that was threatening the species. She told them of the Council of Beasts that had taken the decision to try and save themselves from extinction. She explained the plan to track down the first Seeds of their Collective Memory. She explained the quest for human help, for an Animal Talker, to interpret the clues. She smiled at Spencer as she said this. It could just as easily have been him that the animals had found.

Spencer did not interrupt her. But he understood what Achak had meant when he said the animals were looking for someone like him. The deer had been shot before he had finished his message and Spencer had never known why it was the beasts had wanted him. Now he knew. He wondered for a moment why his polar bear friends had not mentioned the hunt for an Animal Talker. But looking around he could see that Honesty's tale was news to them. Strong-willed, aggressive hunters roaming hundreds of square miles of ice in their search for food – word of the quest for an Animal Talker had not reached the polar bears.

Honesty spoke in a hushed tone of the whale, Kai, who had died carrying the message to her. She explained the clues which had led her to Jade Mountain. And then she looked at the wrecked dogsled and the tracks of huskies in the snow and hung her head.

Spencer guessed, 'You were on your way there?'

'Yes,' Honesty answered. 'Qannik here was helping me. But the dogs got spooked when they found themselves in the midst of a polar bear conference!'

An old polar bear, his fur patchy and his eyes rheumy, said, 'But we have no Collective Memory of these Seeds.'

Honesty looked worried. 'None at all?' she asked.

There were shakes of the head all around.

'Do you think you've got the clues wrong?' asked Spencer.

'I hope not, I don't think so,' said Honesty doubtfully.

The old bear sighed, 'Our numbers have dwindled. Our range is limited. It is possible that our Collective Memory has faded in these dark times.'

Honesty stood up and addressed herself to the bears, 'Do you think you can help me find the Seeds?'

There was complete silence.

She said more urgently, 'I really need your help! Please!'

A young polar bear muttered, 'But we need to fight the oilmen. Not hunt for Seeds for some apes half a world away.'

There were growls of agreement.

Another bear reared up and gestured with his paws to encompass the icy emptiness around them. 'Seeds are no use to us here!'

Spencer said urgently, 'Look, re-foresting the jungles will help the ice. I know it sounds strange but the rainforests help cool the planet.'

There were blank looks all around.

Spencer tried again. 'You know the sea ice is taking longer to reach the shore every winter. Replanting the rainforests will help the ice come back.'

'Man bear, your words are sweet. We bears suffer the loss of the ice. But I do not see how this can be. I fear you are wrong,' said the old bear sadly.

Mother bear said quietly but in a penetrating voice, 'Perhaps we should help because our animal brothers in Borneo have asked it of us.'

A young angry male lashed out with his paw, raking her face with his powerful claws. 'No ape is my brother.' He looked meaningfully at the children, 'And no human either.'

Spencer made an ice pack and held it gently against mother bear's bleeding face. She whimpered a little from the pain.

Honesty was cross. She stamped her foot angrily, lost her footing on an icy patch and ended up flat on her back.

The angry, young male said, 'You want us to help this cub? She is the runt of the litter who cannot even help herself.'

He turned his back on the bears and walked away, stopping to say over his shoulder, 'I am going to find a way to defend the polar bears – without the help of humans.'

The other bears wavered for a moment indecisively and then they all turned and scattered into the darkness.

Soon, only Honesty, Spencer, mother bear and her two cubs remained.

Honesty looked at Spencer sheepishly. 'Sorry,' she said. 'I didn't mean to drive away your friends.'

Spencer turned to mother bear, 'What about you and the kids?' he asked.

'We will help you find the Seeds,' she said.

• • •

A grey wolf rose quietly to his feet and pointed his long, grey-flecked muzzle towards his master. He set off at an easy lope, bushy tail trailing behind him. He had a long way to go and a lot to report.

-twenty nine-

As the rhino expected, the animal teams had benefited hugely from their trial run. The cobras slithered towards their prey, the human camp leaders all over Borneo, with quiet determination. The pythons slid onto branches overhanging the many logging and plantation outposts. They would provide an aerial view of the fighting and sound the retreat if things were going badly. The massed ranks of tigers and elephants, ready and restless, just waited for the blackness of this darkest of nights to engulf the camps. They knew, from their earlier experience, they had to be careful not to start any fires or they would be at the mercy of humans with firesticks. Aside from that, they had licence to inflict mayhem. The orang utan pairs, trained by Orang Tua and Geram, were not expected to have any difficulty finding and detaching the wires from the generators. All around Borneo, in the dark shadows around human camps, the animals waited.

The rhino had a moment of quiet satisfaction. He had organised well. Soon, his revenge for the fate of the two-horned rhinos of Borneo would be complete.

Gajah the pygmy elephant was less sanguine. He whispered to Orang Tua. 'I am worried.'

'About the moon?'

'Yes, I would not have chosen tonight. In two weeks we would not have had to worry about losing cloud cover. What was the rush?'

Orang Tua frowned, 'I agree. But it is too late to pull out. We have to fight.'

The elephant was silent for a moment. Then he touched the orang utan gently on the shoulder with his trunk. 'There is something else.'

'What?'

'The Animal Talker…'

'What about her?'

'She is young. We have sent her on a dangerous quest. A fully grown creature would struggle with what she has been asked to do.'

The elephant sensed rather than saw the ape nod. He continued, 'And we have not told her the truth.'

'The rhino is right,' muttered Orang Tua. 'What choice did we have?'

'I'm not sure. But to sacrifice others for our own gain – isn't that the human thing to do?'

The orang utan never had the chance to reply. The camp was plunged into darkness. It was their cue to attack.

• • •

It took Honesty and Spencer a while to figure out the best way to proceed. Mother bear offered to let them ride on her back. Honesty, with her riding experience, managed quite well but Spencer was unable to find a rhythm and was lucky not to be badly hurt when he fell off.

Next, they tried to ride the two young bears. Spencer was less afraid but the cubs were too exuberant and could not maintain a steady pace. Not even Honesty could hang on as they raced around in excitement.

In desperation, they collected the snapped harnesses and sled. With some careful knotting they strapped the harnesses to the sled. Mother bear gathered the ends in her mouth and the two kids climbed on board. She was easily as strong as a team of huskies and they were soon careering across the ice at a clipping pace. Only the adventurous spirit of the cubs looked likely to overturn them. A few harsh words from their mother calmed them down and they all continued on their way.

Directions were not a problem. The northern lights had disappeared. But a moon, it looked almost full to Honesty, had risen and hung like a large lamp in the sky. By the pale, eerie light it cast – it was a bit like being colour blind, thought Spencer – they could see the distant peaks. The Jade Mountain was the one closest to the sea so the sled team hugged the coast line, sometimes running across the shingle, sometimes straying onto the ice.

There was no conversation. Honesty and Spencer were too busy concentrating on keeping their balance and holding on with numb fingers. The chastened cubs were silent. Their mother was concentrating on not overturning the sled on the uneven surface. Qannik the husky ran alongside with his tongue hanging out. He was an old dog and this was a hard run.

Occasionally, an Arctic fox would see them and freeze with incredulity. Then he would turn and scurry away, their last sight of him would be a bushy white tail disappearing into a hole. A snowy owl swooped down to have a closer look but then thought better of it. She did not want to get mixed up with such an odd bunch. Once, Honesty saw a great herd of caribou grazing inland on the tundra. She nudged Spencer with an elbow and gestured with her head. He looked up, almost lost his balance and went back to hanging on for dear life. Honesty decided not to draw his attention to any more wonders of the Arctic.

For a long time the peaks did not move. They seemed to stay the same size and the same distance away no matter how far the children travelled. But at last their outlines grew clearer against the grey sky and the mountains started to loom larger. No trees grew above the Arctic Circle – so there were no trees on the north-facing side of the mountains. Thick snow and ice, patches of scraggy brush, icy tundra over a layer of permafrost and bare rock were all that was visible. As the sheer size of Jade Mountain became apparent, Honesty's heart sank. The clues did not say where on the mountain the Seeds were hidden. How in the world was she to locate them on this immense rock that reached the skies and wore a wreath of grey clouds around its neck? Had the Collective Memory of the beasts let them down?

They reached the foot of Jade Mountain. The polar bear came to a stop and the children dismounted carefully. Honesty's legs were so stiff that she stumbled and fell. Spencer helped her up, grimacing with pain as blood started to circulate through his numb fingers. Qannik the husky collapsed to the ground. His eyes were closed and his tongue was lolling. Honesty saw that there were bloodstains on the snow where his paws were rubbed raw. Only the bear cubs seemed unfazed.

Honesty summoned up the energy to climb a few rocks. She picked up a piece of stone and struck the surface hard. There was a sound like the crack of a whip and a large sliver of rock snapped off. Honesty's eyes were grey pools of wonder. The inside was dark green with swirling patterns on the grain. It was a piece of jade.

She took the piece down to the others. 'Jade Mountain,' she breathed.

Spencer was bent over double, his hands resting on his knees. Now he said, 'So, where are the Seeds?'

Honesty looked up at the peak towering above them and then towards the sea. Choppy, grey-green waves broke over the rocky mountain edge that stuck out into the waters. The sea was just a broad channel here. It was early winter but the sea ice had spread down from the North Pole and almost reached the mountain. In a few weeks or months, Honesty realised, the ocean would be frozen solid against the mountainside. Now there was a gap for the sea waters to slosh about. She could see, between waves, that the jade was exposed and shining below the water level.

Spencer asked again, 'So where are the Seeds?'

Honesty replied, gazing into the waters, 'I don't know.'

'You don't know!' Spencer was shouting now. 'What do you mean, you don't know? I thought you had clues.'

'I did. I do! And they've got us this far. To the green mountain.'

'It's a big mountain!'

'I know. I thought it might be obvious when we got here.'

'Well, that's planning ahead,' said Spencer sarcastically.

Qannik got to his feet, limped over to Honesty's side and growled warningly at Spencer.

Spencer glared at the two of them and marched over to the sled. They had managed to salvage some of the food and drink before setting out and the children had an impromptu and silent picnic – sitting apart, but throwing angry glances at each other.

The mother bear looked around hungrily and then leapt into the ocean waters. With a few powerful strokes of her front paws, she crossed the channel of open sea and reached the ice floes on the edge of the ice pack. She started sniffing around and they knew she was looking for something to eat. She wandered off and soon disappeared, her white coat blending against the sea ice.

'Tell me the clues again,' said Spencer.

Honesty recited them.

He listened thoughtfully. 'It's a pity the polar bears have no Collective Memory of the Seeds,' he said thoughtfully.

'What about the sea unicorns?' asked Honesty.

'The narwhals? I've never seen one, have you?'

Honesty shook her head emphatically. 'I'd never even heard of such a creature before this quest.'

Spencer scowled. 'I have no idea how we would find one.'

Mother bear interrupted them. She was yelling to them from the ice. They could not make out what she was saying.

The two got up and headed to the edge, careful to avoid the lapping, freezing water. This was not the time to get hypothermia.

Spencer pointed to his ears to indicate to the bear that she was inaudible. The bear reared up in frustration and then plunged back into the water.

They watched her swim quickly towards them, her long snout poking above the water, her powerful body hidden. She clambered onshore and shook herself vigorously. The children were covered with a cold spray and backed away quickly.

Spencer said, 'I'm sorry, we couldn't hear you. What's up?'

A gruff voice from the water said, 'She wanted to introduce you to me.'

Honesty and Spencer took a few steps forward and peered into the sea.

A round, large head was poking out of the water. It looked like a porpoise or a dolphin – except that a long thin spiral horn, at least six feet long, protruded from its forehead.

Mother bear said, 'This is ...'

Honesty breathed the words like a prayer, '... the sea unicorn.'

'How do you do?' asked Spencer politely.

'Fine – until I was almost the lunch of this big lunk-head,' snapped the narwhal.

Mother bear looked sheepish. 'I mistook him for a very big seal under the ice,' she said. 'Luckily, I noticed the horn.'

'Lucky for you!' said the narwhal. 'This horn was just going to impale its first polar bear.'

Honesty said hurriedly, trying to defuse the tension, 'We are so pleased to meet you, Mr. Sea Unicorn.'

The narwhal looked slightly mollified. 'I suppose so,' he said. 'I am quite rare you know.'

'You are a creature of legend,' said Honesty earnestly.

Spencer was too impatient to keep buttering up the short-tempered beast. He said urgently, 'We're on a quest to find the first Seeds. Do you know where they are?'

The narwhal looked offended again. 'Even if I did, why would I tell a human?'

Honesty interrupted them quickly, scowling at Spencer to be quiet. 'Please, sir,' she said in her most courteous voice, 'The orang utans of Borneo sent us on a quest to find the Seeds. The situation for all the great creatures of the world is dire. The clues led us here to Jade Mountain. But the Collective Memory of the beasts tells us that nothing can be done without the unicorns of the sea.'

Spencer snorted and Qannik turned a guffaw into an unconvincing yelp.

The narwhal ignored them. He said to Honesty, 'Why didn't you say so in the first place? Of course I know where the Seeds are.'

He had their attention now.

'You do?' asked Spencer sceptically.

The narwhal bobbed up and down in the choppy waters. 'Of course I do,' he said scornfully. 'Haven't the narwhals been guarding the Seeds for just about the whole of time?'

'You have?' exclaimed Spencer, who was struggling to take what he privately thought looked like a pig with a spike seriously.

'Why do you think I'm hanging around here under the ice, risking death by polar bear, instead of being somewhere fun?' He was looking miffed again as he remembered his encounter with the bear.

'So where are the Seeds?' asked Honesty politely.

'In a narrow tunnel, in a massive cave, on a green mountain.'

'And where's the cave?'

'Below sea level.'

'What?' exclaimed Spencer.

'Yes. Inconvenient for humans, of course. But just maybe

we didn't want you to find it.' The narwhal continued smugly, 'Besides, even if it was above ground, you wouldn't be able to reach the Seeds.'

'Why not?' barked Qannik.

'Because the tunnel it is in will just about take a six foot long spike.' The sea unicorn pirouetted joyfully, his horn cleaving a small whirlpool in the water. 'A horn just like this one!'

'So, will you help us get them?' asked Honesty.

The narwhal's response was interrupted by the sudden descent of a gyrfalcon into their midst.

The grey-brown bird with long pointed wings, a long tail and a hooked beak, perched on a rock, cocked its head to look at them out of one brilliant speckled eye and squawked, 'My, you're a strange bunch!'

'Did you just stop by to be insulting or do you want something?' asked Spencer irritably.

The gyrfalcon was not discomposed by this rudeness. In fact, he did not seem to notice.

'Yes, I do need something. I met a bunch of bald eagles. Apparently all the higher Arctic birds are supposed to be on the lookout for some sort of 'green mountain'. Have you seen it?'

Spencer kicked the sled in disgust. He said, 'You're sitting on it!'

'I beg your pardon?'

'You're wasting our time and you're sitting on the green mountain.'

The gyrfalcon took off abruptly, and came to rest again on the sled. It looked the mountain up and down. 'I see. Well, I'd better get word back to some human child on a quest. She's the one looking for it.'

'That's me,' said Honesty.

The falcon looked at her in surprise. 'Really?'

'Yes!'

'So, you've found it on your own. That is good news. Err … why did you want it?'

They all turned back to the narwhal. He looked at the polar bears, the two human children, the husky and the gyrfalcon.

He said, 'We have never been told how or by whom the Seeds will be claimed. The guardian has to decide whether to release the Seeds. But you guys, you're too weird. Besides, why would the guardian ever release the Seeds to humans?'

Honesty's heart sank right down to her boots. She was conscious of the intense bone-chilling cold and the bleak wintry landscape. She had come so far. So much had been sacrificed. Were they going to fail now?

Honesty begged, 'Mr. Sea Unicorn, I know it seems strange to give the Seeds to humans …'

'Darn right! Last I heard it wasn't animals cutting down the Borneo rainforests.'

She continued, ignoring the interruption, 'But the orang utans were sure that they could not get the Seeds without the help of an Animal Talker.'

'Why would they think that?'

Spencer interrupted, 'Because only an Animal Talker could have worked out the clues ... and only a human could have made it here to ask for them!'

The narwhal said snidely, '*Only a human* ... that's precisely the sort of arrogance that has led to the state of the forests in the first place.'

Honesty glared daggers at Spencer, 'What Spencer meant,' she said, 'is that because of everything Man has done, it would have been very difficult for the beasts to find their way here – there are too few Higher Beasts left and too many man-made obstacles.'

'That might be true enough,' conceded the sea unicorn. 'But just because you're the only ones who could have got here does not mean you should have the Seeds. After all – you might be planning to destroy the Seeds!'

'We would never do that!' exclaimed Honesty. 'We want to help. I promise – we're not like that.'

The narwhal disappeared under the water and then popped back up.

'Well, you would say that, wouldn't you?'

'Look, we've risked our lives to get here. Higher Beasts have already died in the effort. Mother bear has been ostracised by the polar bears for helping us. This girl's Mum is in jail for standing up to the oil people – don't tell us that we're not on your side!' shouted Spencer. 'You just hang around the sea with a butter knife on your nose, calling yourself a guardian of the Seeds – you're not a guardian, you're an obstacle.'

Honesty opened her mouth and shut it again. She couldn't think of anything to say. Spencer had lost his temper and blown it.

There was complete silence except for the lapping of waves against Jade Mountain.

The sea unicorn said in an unexpectedly calm voice, 'Very well, perhaps you are in earnest – but I cannot give you the Seeds … unless you pass the test.'

'What test?' asked Honesty in surprise.

• • •

A King Cobra slithered through the undergrowth quietly. He had almost reached the caravan. The only sound to be heard was the air-conditioning unit vibrating. The hot air it expelled did not bother the passing snake. The cobra, pale scales almost invisible against the cream-coloured vehicle, slid up the steps and across a window sill. It was open a crack, more than enough for a creature adept at flattening its long body to squeeze into tight places. The snake could see a figure under the covers on a bunk raised just off the floor. It slid forward slowly. The cold air in the caravan was making it sleepy as it slithered under the blankets looking for its prey. To the snake's surprise, it could not sense the warm blood or regular breathing of a sleeping human.

Suddenly, the covers were ripped off the bed, revealing pillows that were bunched up to look like a man. The exposed cobra reared up and with its hood flared, scanned the cramped quarters for danger. The man who should have been on the bed struck hard with a machete. The cobra's head was severed by the first blow. It lay in a pool of blood on the bed. The snake's body continued to writhe and twist for many minutes afterwards.

Outside, the orang utans did their work well. The moment the lights went out, the elephants and tigers rushed into the camp, pulling out tent pegs and overturning vehicles. But no bleary-eyed, panicky humans came stumbling out. Instead a shrill whistle sounded that hurt the ears. Men ran out of their tents and caravans carrying firesticks. The beasts charged at them – confident they would not be able to see to shoot. They were wrong.

In the darkness, the humans could see.

Now they turned their guns on the creatures.

The rhino could not understand it. He screamed a retreat and charged back into the jungle. The few who had survived followed him.

• • •

The narwhal said, 'It's quite a simple riddle, really. Are you ready?'

The children agreed grimly. What choice did they have?

'A human has to take a grizzly bear, a moose, and a shrub across a river. He can only take one of the three across at a time. If he takes the shrub, the grizzly will eat the moose. If he takes the grizzly, the moose will eat the shrub. How does he get the three across the river?'

Honesty and Spencer looked at the narwhal blankly.

'But we have no idea!' protested Honesty.

'No idea, no Seeds,' said the sea unicorn, waving his horn at them smugly and slipping back into the sea.

Hours later, the children were still at a loss. The sun came up, a huge golden orb on a low trajectory on the horizon, casting a thin light over their predicament. Spencer was on his knees in the snow drawing diagrams with a piece of jade. Every now and then, he would scrub out his drawings with a mitten and start over. Honesty had almost given up trying. She sat back on her haunches, thinking of Kai and only looking up when Spencer demanded she look at his latest attempt to solve the problem. A quick shake of the head and a muttered, 'That moose is *so* dead,' would send him back to the drawing board.

Qannik was on the sled a couple of feet away. His muzzle rested on his front paws as he watched their efforts sleepily.

Spencer asked him irritably, 'Do you have any idea what the answer is?'

The dog raised his head to look at him and then barked a quick negative. He remarked, 'The answer requires logic. Animals are very bad at logic, I'm afraid.'

'So is this human,' scowled Spencer.

'Where's mother bear?' asked Honesty.

'Looking for something other than narwhal to eat if she knows what's good for her,' said the narwhal, putting in one of his periodic appearances. 'Any luck yet?' he asked.

The children shook their heads in unison.

Honesty asked in a small voice, 'You're sure you won't give us the Seeds?'

'Rules are rules, honey!' the sea beast said in an almost kindly tone.

The gyrfalcon who had been soaring above their heads, descended into their midst and asked, 'Any luck yet?'

Spencer shook his head curtly.

He went back to his drawings and Honesty watched mother bear who was dragging a seal carcass across the ice with her two cubs prancing around her. She dragged it to the water's edge and settled down to a meal. The cubs tucked in as well, occasionally mock growling and snarling at each other over a choice tidbit, practising for when they might have to defend dinner against other polar bears and Arctic scavengers.

Mother bear looked up and saw Honesty watching them. She said something to her cubs, Honesty could not hear it, and swum vigorously across the channel. As she got closer, she asked, 'Any luck yet?'

Honesty shook her head. Spencer ignored the question although it was obvious from his stiff back that he had heard it.

Mother bear asked politely, 'Would either of you like some seal?'

Again Honesty shook her head and Spencer ignored the question – but Qannik whimpered.

'Would *you* like some?' asked mother bear, addressing the husky.

Qannik barked a sharp, 'Yes,' and then whined, 'But I can't swim over there! I am not strong enough.'

Mother bear said, 'I will bring you some.'

She was as good as her word. She swum back to the cubs, chased them away from the seal remnants, tore off a chunk with her huge teeth and plunged back into the water. She clambered out and lay the meat near Qannik who fell on it ravenously.

Mother bear, panting a little from her exertions, plunged back into the icy waters and paddled powerfully to the cubs.

Honesty watched her climb out the other side, shake herself energetically and go back to her meal. She felt the faintest stirring of an idea and looked at Spencer.

She said, 'Spencer,' and when he kept working, 'Spencer!'

The boy looked up.

'I think I've got it!'

It took them a while to work out the details but in the end they were confident.

They stood on the water's edge and yelled for the narwhal.

When he poked his round head out of the water, Spencer said, 'The human takes the moose across the water. He goes back for the shrub and takes that across …'

The narwhal said smugly, 'But the moose would eat the shrub.'

Spencer shook his head, 'No, because when he gets the shrub across, he brings the moose back. Then he takes the grizzly across, leaves the grizzly with the shrub and goes back for the moose!'

The narwhal looked thoughtful.

Honesty said, 'That must be right!'

The sea unicorn said, 'I think, you know, that might very well be the answer.'

Spencer asked in disbelief, 'Don't you know?'

The narwhal looked sheepish, 'Forgotten actually!' He changed the subject, 'But how did you get it?'

'It was Honesty,' said Spencer happily.

'I was watching mother bear go back and forth across the channel,' said Honesty modestly, 'And I suddenly realised that there was no reason that she couldn't be carrying something both ways!'

The narwhal said, 'Well … looks like you're the real thing. I'll get the Seeds.'

It took a few seconds for the sea beast's words to sink in. Then Spencer let out a whoop of delight and thumped Honesty on the back. 'We did it,' he shouted. 'We did it!'

It took a surprisingly short time to retrieve the Seeds after that. The land animals waited on the rocks of Jade Mountain. The narwhal took a deep breath and disappeared under the water. He returned half an hour later with a block of ice on the end of his horn. He swam as near to the shore as he could. The children grabbed the slippery block and yanked on it. They could not get a grip. Their fingers kept slipping.

Spencer looked hard at the narwhal's horn with its spiral design. He said, 'We need to unscrew it!' He leaned over the water's edge again and started turning the block anti-clockwise. Honesty scrambled forward to help him. The ice block came off. The children staggered back under its weight. They dropped it on the ground and sank down to their knees around it. Deep inside, visible through the layers of ice, were the Seeds.

'It's brilliant!' said Honesty. 'They've been preserved in ice all this while.'

'But we need to get them out,' Spencer said, ever practical. 'We can't carry a block of ice all the way back.'

The polar bear solved the problem of how to melt a block of ice in below freezing temperatures. She lay down and scooped the block between her front paws and then laid her chin on it. Her body warmth soon began to melt the ice. Rivulets of water rolled down its sides. The frosty ice became translucent and then melted, slowly at first and then quickly. And one by one, the Seeds fell out until a small heap of about a hundred Seeds lay on the ground. Honesty scooped them up, careful to leave none behind. She emptied out their sandwich box and put in the Seeds. Then she put the box back into her small knapsack.

She grinned at the rest. 'Time to go home,' she said.

They were all concentrating on the Seeds. No one noticed

a rumbling in the far distance. If they had, they would have most likely put it down to the sound of a blizzard far away. But now, in the silence after Honesty had given words to the longing in their hearts, they all heard it.

-thirty-

'It's a helicopter,' said Spencer. As he spoke, the machine came roaring over the mountainside and landed with a churning of snow and mud, two hundred yards from them. Honesty clutched the bag of Seeds to her chest. The rotors came to a stop. Three men and a wolf jumped out. It was Valentine, Mr. Deakin and Spencer's Dad.

The men walked over. The wolf slunk forward too, keeping close to Valentine. Spencer noticed that Mr. Deakin had a gun. He stepped in front of the bears.

When they were close enough to be heard without shouting, Dad, his face pale and frightened, said, 'Move away very slowly, son.'

Mr. Deakin cocked his gun and aimed it at mother bear.

'Son, you and your friend, move away from the bear.'

Spencer realised it was all a complete misunderstanding. Dad thought that Honesty and he were in danger from the polar bears. He said, 'It's alright, Dad. They're my friends.' And he took a step back and put his arm around mother bear's neck.

His father lurched forward and then stopped, unsure what to do, afraid to provoke the bears.

Valentine said, and his voice was as cold as a glacier, 'I want the Seeds.'

Spencer's Dad said, 'What?'

'They know what I mean.'

Honesty said bravely, her chin in the air, 'You can't have them.'

'What are you talking about?' shouted Spencer's Dad angrily.

'They have the first Seeds. I want them.'

'But how did you find out about the Seeds?' It was Spencer who asked the question.

Tarzan the wolf answered in a wicked growl, 'I told him. I overheard you talking to the bears. And I told him.'

The children looked confused.

'But that means …,' Honesty's voice trailed off uncertainly.

Valentine laughed. 'Yes, you're not the only Animal Talkers around here.' And then his face grew angry and he spat at the ground in disgust.

Spencer said, 'But the Seeds are to re-forest Borneo and the other rainforests. It will save the animals!'

'Now why would I want to do that?' asked Valentine rudely.

'But … ,' Honesty struggled for words to express her feelings, 'If we can talk to the animals, it shows we are not that different, animals and people.'

'Not that different, perhaps,' said Valentine, 'but beasts

are our enemies!'

'How can you say that?' asked Spencer angrily, remembering Achak. 'We slaughter them. They don't harm us.'

'Well, that just shows how wrong you are, young man. Just yesterday, animals attacked my plantation camps in Borneo,' remarked Valentine. 'And it's not the first time either. They killed twenty of my men the first time. But this time we were ready.'

'What do you mean?' asked Honesty in a small voice.

'That Seeds or no Seeds, it might be too late for your Borneo friends ... my men had night vision goggles!'

Honesty was shocked, 'But why would the animals attack humans?'

'Because they know, like I do – that this is war – a war for the resources of this planet. So whose side are you on? You need to decide, like I did. A bunch of furry animals or your family, your friends, *humans*?'

Spencer was furious, 'It's not a choice between animals and humans. If the Borneo animals attacked, they must have had a good reason, like to protect their homes. We could share the planet if it wasn't for people like you!'

Valentine chuckled, 'I'm planning on cutting down every last tree in Borneo.' He glanced at the polar bears, 'And sucking out every last drop of oil from this ice.'

'But why?' asked Spencer. 'Why can't you leave the beasts some space?'

'Ah, but you don't quite understand, young man. It's

business. I'm a very rich man and I like it that way. Besides, I want the beasts dead. Every single Higher Beast. Except for my friend Tarzan here, of course. But then, he's almost human.' The wolf chuckled at this.

Spencer's face showed his bewilderment. Honesty said, 'But if you're an Animal Talker …'

Valentine's voice grew hot and screechy. 'Am I an *animal* to speak to beasts? No! I will kill them all rather than hear their words.' He calmed down. 'Getting stinking rich in the process is great too, of course.'

There was a silence.

Spencer broke it. 'Well, you're bonkers, aren't you?'

Honesty added, 'Just like Ahab.'

Valentine screamed, 'Enough of this nonsense. Give me the Seeds!'

'What are you going to do with them?' Spencer asked.

'Destroy them, of course.'

Honesty was pale but determined. 'Never,' she said firmly.

Mr. Deakin raised his gun again.

'Hand them over or the bear dies,' said Valentine.

Mother bear laughed.

The children stood firm.

A shot rang out and mother bear collapsed. The children fell to their knees beside her.

As quick as lightning, Tarzan leapt forward and seized the knapsack from Honesty, whose fingers were slack from the shock. Only Qannik was alert. He sprang for the wolf.

His great husky jaws clamped around the grey throat. They fought furiously, wolf and dog. Mr. Deakin raised his gun again but he could not get a clear shot.

Qannik was an old dog and Tarzan a wolf in his prime. It was only the fact that the wolf had the knapsack between his teeth that kept him from using his strength to kill Qannik. Qannik knew, as animals do when they enter a fight to the death, he could not win. He glanced around desperately. Mother bear was lying in a pool of blood. Her cubs were whimpering around her. The children were wide-eyed and aghast.

Qannik feinted, as if he was going for the throat again. Instead, he exposed his flank. It was too tempting for the wolf. Tarzan dropped the knapsack and seized the husky in a death grip, every fang plunged into the dog's side. But Qannik had a plan. He grabbed the knapsack and with one last incredible effort, pitched himself and the wolf backwards into the water. They sank below the surface and then popped back up, a few yards apart. Qannik had released the knapsack with the Seeds as he fell in. The bag was waterlogged and starting to sink. Qannik barked, 'Falcon!'

The gyrfalcon took off and dived for the bag. Her talons curled to seize the knapsack. Tarzan spotted the danger and paddled furiously. Honesty's heart was in her mouth. The wolf was going to get to the bag before the falcon. And then the wolf stopped abruptly. He went stiff.

'It's the narwhal!' shouted Spencer. And it was. He had pierced the wolf through the heart with his horn.

Valentine's howl of rage echoed around the mountains.

The falcon, wings beating strongly, lifted the soaking bag into the air. A single Seed fell out and landed at their feet.

But they had forgotten Mr. Deakin. With one trained hunter's action he raised his gun and sighted the bird.

'Dad!' yelled Spencer.

Spencer's Dad who had stood like a statue throughout, unable to comprehend the enormity of what was unfolding before him, jerked into action. He leapt for Mr. Deakin, catching his arm just as he pulled the trigger. He knocked the gun out of his hands. It went off. Spencer's Dad fell back clutching his shoulder. The gun spun across the icy, slippery surface into the sea.

The gyrfalcon was only a speck on the horizon now. Valentine watched it go. He looked into the water where narwhal, husky and wolf had all disappeared without a trace.

He looked at Spencer's Dad, lying on the ground and clutching his shoulder, his son hovering protectively.

He said, 'You're fired.'

Valentine beckoned to Mr. Deakin and they walked away towards the helicopter.

• • •

Mother bear was alive, just. They sat with her and her cubs. She opened her eyes long enough to whisper, 'Do not weep for me. It was an honour to help my fellow beasts.' Her eyes shut for the last time.

The narwhal, who had come back to pay his respects, saluted them briefly with his horn and then turned and swam away. The children said goodbye to the two polar bear cubs. Honesty cried but Spencer was stony-faced as they hugged the young beasts who assured them that they were old enough to fend for themselves. And it did seem that they had matured in that same twinkling of an eye that had taken their mother from them.

The children had got to their feet for the long trek back when Ataneq appeared with a team of dogs. He had followed Spencer's tracks through the night, worried about the boy.

'What happened?' he asked.

No one answered. The gyrfalcon had saved the Seeds, for the time being at least. But the price they had paid was so high.

As they got ready to leave, Spencer turned to look at his polar bear friend one last time.

Suddenly, he ran back towards the body. The others followed him more slowly.

'Look,' he said in a voice filled with awe.

The Seed that had fallen out of the bag as the gyrfalcon flew away – it was sprouting. As they watched, small green leaves began to unfurl.

Mother bear was soon lying under the shade of the only tree north of the Arctic Circle.

-THE END-

If you would like to find out what happens to the Seeds, the children and the Higher Beasts as they continue to battle Valentine and his evil plans, please look out for :

BOOK TWO OF
'THE ANIMAL TALKERS'

-about the author-

Shamini Flint lives in Singapore with her husband and two children. She is an ex-lawyer, ex-lecturer, stay-at-home mum and writer.

Shamini has written numerous children's picture books including "Jungle Blues", "Turtle Takes a Trip" and "A T-Rex Ate my Homework". She is also the author of the highly-acclaimed "Sasha" series of children's travel books.

Shamini's first three crime novels, "Inspector Singh Investigates — A Most Peculiar Malaysian Murder", "Inspector Singh Investigates — A Bali Conspiracy Most Foul" and "Inspector Singh Investigates — The Singapore School of Villainy" are published by Little, Brown.

Shamini's website is www.shaminiflint.com.

Children's novels by Shamini Flint

Diary of a Soccer Star
Diary of a Cricket God
Ten
The Seeds of Time

Available on www.sunbearpublishing.com
and www.amazon.co.uk.